I0617656

Where There's a Will
My Heart to Keep

Leopard's Spots
Levi
Oscar
Timothy
Isaiah
Gilbert
Esau
Sullivan
Wesley
Nischal
Justice
Sabin
Cliff

Mossy Glenn Ranch
Chaps and Hope
Ropes and Dreams
Saddles and Memories
Fences and Freedom
Riding and Regrets
Broncs and Bullies
Hay and Heartbreak
Vaqueros and Vigilance

Spotless
Hide
Hunt
Home
Heart

Coyote's Call
Off Course
In from the Cold
Blue Moon Rising

Valen's Pack
Run with the Moon
Exodus

YES, FOREVER

BAILEY BRADFORD

YES, FOREVER

Dedication

There is no shame in making mistakes. Forgive yourself. Love yourself.

Chapter One

San Antonio was home, but there were some days when John Weston wished he lived somewhere else. Somewhere cooler, with less humidity and perhaps not governed by a man determined to stomp all over John's rights. When work was stressful, or on the nights he was so lonely he couldn't sleep, John often fantasized about moving to a different city. He thought about San Francisco, or LA, New York or even Miami or Amsterdam. He didn't know any more about those cities than the average person, but in his mind, they were bustling, gay-friendly places teeming with available, attractive men.

John wasn't stupid — he knew the difference between fantasy and reality, but they were *his* fantasies. If he wanted to imagine himself lusted after by innumerable sexy men while he spent a restless night in bed, then that's what he would do. Besides, when it came down to it, he wouldn't leave San Antonio. His family was here, his parents, sisters and brother. Without their love and support, he'd have been lost a long time ago in the morass of depression and hopelessness that had once claimed him.

It was with their help that he'd been dragged, at first unwillingly but then gratefully, out of the mess in his head. It was with their love that he'd come to accept, as much as he could, that he had bouts of depression and likely always would. 'Mental illness' — John hated those words, not because they indicated he was at fault, but because so many people attached other labels to them, like 'crazy' and 'psychotic'. He was neither of those things, but he did have chemicals in his brain that at times misfired or became unbalanced somehow and sent him into a tailspin. Knowing it wasn't his fault, that he had a disease like any other kind of disease people could get, didn't really help. His family did. They reassured him that he wasn't defined by those two words, any more than his father was defined by his diabetes or his mother by the breast cancer she'd survived. Without his family, John was sure he'd have been so very lost. Perhaps not a stereotype, but still, lost.

Thinking of his family made days like the one John had just had bearable. His boss had been on a tear, snapping at everyone. John hadn't been an exception. Generally, Mr. Stiles was a nice enough man. A little standoffish, but John understood that since he was the boss and didn't want to be taken advantage of, should he be too friendly with his employees.

The carpet designing company John had worked for since graduating high school was rapidly growing after years of struggling through the faltering economy. With the discovery of the Eagle Ford Shale in Texas, hotels, motels and apartments were being built at what John assumed must be record rates. They all wanted durable, attractive carpeting with vibrant patterns in some areas and soothing tones in sleeping rooms.

With the influx of oil company execs, oil field workers and their families, everything was close to booming in the area. Restaurants and other businesses were being opened in small towns that had only had a Dairy Queen before, if they were lucky, along with the usual mom and pop places.

After six years working at Carpets Galore, John had moved up the ladder and was now in charge of putting together the designs and actual sales. He'd come a long way from a grunt carpet hauler. But not far enough to escape Mr. Stiles' temper when there were contracts verging on being unfulfilled because one of their carpet suppliers hadn't shipped their order.

John shrugged as he walked out to his truck. The sun would set soon, but until then, it was hot—miserably so, as usual in mid-August. It'd be hot at night, too, but at least the sunlight wouldn't be beating down on him, threatening to cook him alive.

The door handle on his Tundra was so hot that John halfway expected to see some skin stuck to it when he tugged the door open. He knew that he wouldn't actually lose any skin to the handle but damn, it was uncomfortable to touch. He leaned in and stuck the key in the ignition, chiding himself mentally for not having splurged on the remote start option. He could have had the AC going already if he had.

The truck was John's pride and joy. It was the first thing he'd really bought on his own. He patted the dash, even though it too was hotter than all get out, and got in the truck. Ice cold air blasted his face. John shut the truck door and sighed happily, glad for the weekend ahead. The seat was too warm for comfort, but the chilly air was perfect. The combination of the two sensations was sending his body into a tailspin—sweat breaking out on his back and neck while the front of him was beginning to get goosebumps here and there.

"This is nice." He really did love his truck. John's stomach growled and he closed his eyes for a moment, savoring the freedom of two days off. Other single people might be making wild plans, or exciting plans involving clubs and hookups—heck, even Craigslist and hookups—but John just wanted to unwind, maybe go hiking at Lost Maples or canoeing down the Guadalupe River. The beach would be great, too. There'd be a crowd almost anywhere he went to escape the city, but it'd still be nice to get away for a little while and be outside.

Craigslist and clubs just weren't for him. John had never tried the former, though admittedly he had looked at their M4M section. Sometimes it provided some spank material every bit as lewd as what he found on porn sites. Another source for fantasies that John knew would never be good in reality. He didn't trust himself at clubs, because a few drinks made him stupid and reckless, and he really wasn't supposed to be drinking with the antidepressants he was on. Loneliness was familiar and safe, even if it did suck at times.

Besides which, he had friends he could hang out with if he wanted to. Most of them liked clubs or had paired up with a significant other, though, and John didn't care to feel like the awkward third wheel. Although, maybe he would call and see if Henry wanted to hit up the beach or hike this weekend. It had been a while since John had got to hang out with his best buddy.

John shook his head. He needed to stop letting his mind drift—no easy task, but he managed. The parking lot was empty by the time he put the truck in gear and headed out onto the street.

Traffic on Interstate 37 was a mess, the usual afternoon commute hell made even worse by a wreck that everyone gawked at. John refused to look on principle — it irked him to no end that people slowed down to stare. He knew it didn't make him better than the oglers, but he still felt a little spurt of self-righteousness that might have made him a dick. *No one's perfect.* John wasn't going to castigate himself over it.

It took him an hour to get to his apartment. When there was no traffic, he could get home in fifteen minutes without speeding. John was wrung-out when he parked his truck, his nerves pinging and his hands aching from gripping the steering wheel. Twice, he'd almost been hit by some idiot cutting in front of him, or trying to. The second time, the guy would have broadsided John had he not blared the horn. How anyone could have not seen his red Tundra was beyond him, but it didn't matter in the end. He hadn't been hit, and he didn't have to drive anywhere else tonight unless he wanted to.

John got out of the truck and hit the lock and alarm buttons. The sun was almost set now, but he still felt like he'd be melting into the asphalt if he didn't get inside. Luckily, the interior of the building was pleasantly cool. John wiped off his brow and waved at Mrs. Royal.

"Do you have plans for the weekend?" she asked, patting her short gray hair.

John caught the message quickly. "No, ma'am, not specifically, although I was toying around with the idea of hitting up the beach or something like that." He squinted and hoped he looked surprised. "Did you…did you get your hair cut? Because you look more beautiful than usual, and I would swear your hair was longer yesterday." He really couldn't tell, but he liked Mrs. Royal. She was sweet and kind.

She patted her hair again and beamed at him. "Why yes, I did, you flirt. Mr. Marks even noticed."

John didn't have to fake his smile at that. "He did, huh? Well, well, what plans do *you* have this weekend?"

Mrs. Royal had been trying to get Mr. Marks' attention for weeks without being blatantly obvious. John wasn't sure the man was good enough for Mrs. Royal, but as long as she was happy, that was what was important.

"I—" She stopped and folded her hands together over the slight swell of her belly. "Well, I was wondering, do you think it would be too forward for me to ask Mr. Marks to Sunday dinner? You know I take it at the Baptist church down the street."

"It's great that the church does that," John said, even though he'd never step foot in the place. Religion gave him hives. He was working on his spiritual beliefs as he went along in life. "And no, I don't think it would be too forward. Mr. Marks would probably enjoy getting out and having a meal with you, and at least one of us would have a date." He winked when a blush delicately tinted her cheeks pink. "Maybe you can tell me how that's done, give me some pointers."

Mrs. Royal tittered and shook her head. "Well, you won't be finding your prince charming in your apartment, unless there is something to those Internet dating sites. Personally, I think the old fashioned way is best. Nothing beats seeing someone out in public and having your heart flutter, your pulse race because they touch something inside of you."

"Yes, ma'am," John agreed, though he had no idea what that felt like. Honestly, it sounded like the reaction he'd had to Ecstasy the one time he'd tried it years ago. *Minus the sweat and panic and fear that I was dying, of course.* "I've never tried those match-making sites. I'm only twenty-five. If I don't find the perfect man by the time I'm thirty, then I might have to reconsider them."

"Oh, you'll find him, or better yet, he'll find you." Mrs. Royal fluttered her hands in his direction. "I don't see how anyone could resist falling in love with you."

John almost laughed at that, but he didn't want to hurt Mrs. Royal's feelings. He had a mirror, though, and knew he was just an average-looking guy. No one would think there was anything special about his brown eyes and brown hair. He was just one six-foot tall, walking earth tone—shades of brown from his head to the fuzz on his calves.

"Thank you, Mrs. Royal. Be sure and let me know how Sunday goes." John leaned closer and whispered loudly, "And if Mr. Marks needs a talking to, you let me know. I'll make sure he knows how to treat a lady. I may not date women, but my parents certainly taught me how to be a gentleman."

"Oh, you dear young man." She touched his cheek then giggled. "Go on, I know you must want to get out of that suit. My Reggie always wanted his off as soon as he clocked out."

"Yes, ma'am." John waved again and darted to the stairwell. His apartment was on the third floor, and John never took the elevator. Not even when he bought groceries, which kept him from over-buying, because trotting up and down three flights of stairs could suck at times.

Today, he enjoyed the mini-workout. It felt good to make it to his door and not be short-winded, like he had been the first few weeks he'd made that trek. The hallway was empty. John was on friendly enough terms with everyone on his floor, even if he didn't know all their names. He was lucky in that he'd never had bad neighbors, and he strived to be a good one himself, saying hello and offering to help them if he saw they might need it.

Tonight he slipped inside his apartment and began stripping as soon as he'd closed and locked his door. He hung his tie, suit coat and slacks up in the closet by the small entryway. His shoes were put in their usual spot as well. The rest of his clothes — shirt, undershirt and socks — he put in the hamper, then he was going to sprawl in his boxers in front of the TV for a while.

One frozen dinner and a soda later, John was watching a program on classic cars when his cell phone rang. John reached for it, slapping at the couch, not looking away from the beautiful Barracuda he'd almost ditch his truck for. When he grabbed the phone, he took a second to glance at the display then grinned at the oddness of Henry calling him just then.

"Hey, man, I was thinking about you just a little while ago," John opened with, glad to hear from his friend. "How've you been?"

"Busy as fuck, but that's not an excuse for not returning your call sooner." Henry sounded contrite, and possibly worried he'd hurt John's feelings. John could fix that.

"It's no problem, I've been working my butt off too, and I always could have called, texted or emailed again. It's not like you're not on my Facebook, either." Henry was the one friend who really knew him, knew about the depression that had at times knocked John on his ass. All the other friends who knew about it had dropped off the edge of the world when John had had a bad spell. He'd been unable to find the energy to chat or visit with them, and they had long since returned the favor, removing him from their lives.

It was hurtful, John knew that, but he hadn't been able to function beyond work and caring for himself. Henry had waited patiently, leaving him messages and emails and other various supporting statements. Henry understood depression, how it could take hold of a person and cut them off from everything and everyone, even if the person fought it. The man was truly a priceless friend.

"Yeah, but still." Henry sighed gustily and John winced. "It's been one thing or another, and best friends shouldn't be out of touch for so long. You got plans for the weekend?"

"Nah." John was grinning again, stupid-happy. "I was thinking this afternoon that I'd call and see if you wanted to hang out somewhere. Beach, hiking, canoeing — whatever you want, man, it's your call."

"Great minds and all of that," Henry replied after chuckling. "I need a John fix, my friend. How about we go to Mathis, camp out and just spend the weekend escaping the city?"

"Sounds great. When do you want to leave?" John asked, sitting up straight, his week's worth of work-related exhaustion vanishing under the promise of an adventure with his friend.

"Now," Henry answered, "but I know we can't. Have to pack and all of that."

John glanced at his watch. It was just after eight. "I can be packed and out the door in half an hour. We can stop, pick up supplies at the store, then be in Mathis before eleven or twelve, if you want. I'm game." *And concerned, because Henry sounds so weary.* "Has anything happened that I should know about, or that you want to tell me?" Pushing wasn't his thing, but he would make the offer to listen. He really wanted to know if something was wrong with Henry, or in Henry's life.

Henry sighed again, and John shifted on the couch, ready to get up and go to Henry's place. His friend wasn't prone to theatrics, and that had been quite a noisy, miserable sound.

"I'll tell you about it when we're on the road," Henry said right about the time John was going to give up on getting an answer. "Suffice it to say, I'm giving up on men, for good this time."

John had heard Henry joke about that several times before, but he seemed to be serious now. "Do I need to kick someone's ass for you?"

Henry snickered at that, but John didn't take any offense. Henry had a good three inches on him in height and fifty pounds or so in muscle. The man was the most sought-after physical trainer in the gym he worked at. He could beat most guys to a pulp with one hand.

"Thanks, but I'd rather you not go to prison for me. The guilt, you know. It'll make me wrinkle."

"Goof," John got out before laughing. "All right, give me half an hour then I'll be at your curb, ready to whisk you away for the weekend."

"Deal. And, John?"

John hesitated in mid-step, as if moving would somehow halt the conversation. "Yeah?"

"Thanks." Henry hung up then, and John snorted at his own weirdness, standing with one foot barely touching the floor. He tossed the phone back on the couch and went about getting ready for a guys' camping weekend. That included filling the ice chest up with soda and bottled water. He saw no reason to buy more when he already had plenty on hand.

Once he'd packed up what snacks he could find, John quickly set about picking out clothes. Shorts, tanks, T-shirts and a pair of jeans, along with underwear and socks, then he was done with the clothing part. A trip to the bathroom and he had everything gathered. John wished he'd showered when he'd first got home, but he shrugged off the regret. They'd both be smelling pretty ripe by the end of each day, what with the heat and all. Luckily, there were showers available where they would camp out.

John made sure his medicine was packed too, then he dressed in his favorite worn jeans and a soft T-shirt. He pulled on thick socks before slipping his feet into his hiking boots. A beige baseball cap completed his outfit, and he was ready to go.

Almost. John stopped by the couch, spotting his phone. He set down the bag he was carrying and went back to get his phone charger. Then he called his mother.

"John, how are you?" she asked right off the bat.

"Fine, Mom. Is everyone good?" He'd just seen them two nights ago when he'd gone to the weekly family dinner. Talk about chaos. There'd been kids screaming and laughing, adults bickering and teasing—John loved it, loved his family.

"Oh yes, everyone's fine. Are you calling with some good news?"

John picked up on the not so subtle hint. His mother had been after him to find a nice guy for a year or so now, since all his other siblings had tied the knot. Pointing out that he hadn't been allowed to do the same by law until just recently made no difference to her. "It's the commitment that counts, not a piece of paper," she'd said with a great deal of exasperation. Then she'd promptly begun listing places and dating services she thought he should use to find the perfect man. And she always asked him if he'd started dating anyone whenever they talked. It was often her first question.

"No, Mom, I haven't magically met Mr. Right since Wednesday," he told her with as much patience as he could muster. "I know you and Dad met and made googly eyes at each other and instantly fell in love, but y'all are the exception, not the rule. The rest of us have to suffer through a line of No Ways before we meet our Yes, Forever."

"I don't know who fed you that line of bull, but it wasn't me or your dad," his mother informed him. "There's nothing wrong with waiting for that one special person instead of having sex with anyone who's willing. If I'd been easy, your dad would never have thought past getting in my pants, and once he'd done that, he'd have been long gone."

John would have been offended at the implication that he was on the slutty side, except that wasn't what his mother meant, and she'd given all her kids that same speech numerous times. "Well, Mom, I haven't found anyone willing to have sex with me lately anyway—"

She gasped, and he chuckled. "You brought sex up first. Like I was saying, there's no one chasing after me and if there was, I wouldn't be jumping into the sack with him. I might not have gotten the lesson the first few times you told it, but I get it now."

"Obviously not if you aren't getting out where you can meet anyone. Why, there's a church over by Olmos Park that welcomes everyone and I bet you'd meet several nice young men there."

"Gee, what would I do with several of them, hmm?" he teased.

His mother let out an indignant sound. "John Wayne Weston! You'd better watch that mouth of yours, or you'll be missing a piece of pecan pie next Wednesday!"

"Yes, ma'am, sorry," he quickly apologized. His mother's desserts were not to be missed — they were truly one of life's treasures. "I'll think about the church, seriously, but I just wanted to let you know that Henry and I are heading to Mathis for the weekend. Cell service is iffy there, but if you need to reach us, you can leave a message at the camp ground's headquarters."

"Is it the same number as it was last time y'all went a few months ago?"

"Should be, but if it isn't, I'll call tomorrow and update it with you. Love you, Mom."

"Love you too, son. Be safe and have fun. And think about that church."

She hung up, and John did too. He hefted his duffle bag and tucked his phone in his front pocket. Then he took the handle of the ice chest, glad it was a wheeled one rather than one he would have to carry outright. However, he wasn't going to be taking the stairs this time. He'd likely run over himself with the ice chest and end up breaking his neck.

It was dark outside, the late summer sun setting a little after eight. John made his way to this truck and was on the road to Henry's in no time. Henry lived on the south side of San Antonio, in a neighborhood that had seen better days. It wasn't a bad area, just run down. The houses had a dated, 1960s look to them that could only be altered by a complete renovation on the outside, and in Henry's case, the inside as well.

John pulled up outside and was in the middle of texting Henry that he was there when a loud thump on the driver's side window startled a yelp out of him.

"Shit," he breathed as his heart galloped back down from his throat. Henry smirked at him through the glass. "Asshole," John muttered, but he was damned happy to see Henry. John unlocked the doors. Were those dark circles ringing Henry's eyes, or had that been the bad lighting? He waited until Henry opened the passenger door, having tossed his bag in the truck bed. Those were definitely dark circles under his friend's eyes, bruising that pale skin.

"I know, I look like shit," Henry said as soon as he hopped in the truck. "I haven't been sleeping much. I think I fucked up something that could have been really good, and I don't think I can fix it."

"Oh." John glanced at Henry again. "I thought it was the other way around." It usually was, with Henry picking one loser after another, each of them dumping on him and leaving him heartbroken, or at least with a battered ego. "Want to tell me what happened?"

Henry groaned and buckled up. "Yeah, of course I don't." He laughed. "You'll say that I'm a total idiot who doesn't deserve Cory, and I have to agree."

"I'll never agree to that if he's a good guy. You deserve someone who treats you right."

Another groan was Henry's response, at first. John waited patiently, driving while Henry remained silent until finally blurting out, "Cory was great, John. Nice, built, attractive but not that model-gorgeous type. He wasn't a jerk like all the others. He wanted a real relationship, wanted to take it slow and let us build something together if we could. But I guess we—no, I— couldn't, because I went out and…and I didn't mean to, but…"

John's stomach cramped because he feared he knew where this was going. It didn't stop him from asking, "What happened?"

"He wanted to take it slow, so we had been. No sex, and oh my God, did that suck. I got mad, because who *does* that, John? Huh? Who doesn't want to fucking get laid?" Henry growled. He smacked the dash.

"Hey, don't abuse the truck," John said, not joking at all. "I'm sorry you're upset, but I don't want a busted dash."

"Right. Right, sorry. I know this is your baby." Henry caressed the spot he'd hit. "But seriously, John, wouldn't you have thought that he was stringing you along if you'd been me, after all the jackasses I've dated?"

John shook his head. "I'd like to think I would have asked him, had a conversation about it all. It's been so long since I've even dated anyone, though, that I honestly couldn't tell you what I'd have done in your place." Not cheat, that was certain, but he wouldn't judge his friend. Henry had been treated like shit by every guy he'd dated, and John figured that had to be a hard mold to break out of. "It sounds like you were trying to strike out first."

"I was fucking stupid." Henry sighed. "I went out, blew a guy, got a hand job that was mediocre at best, and lost the one man who'd ever treated me like I was worth something. I think I need a brain transplant."

"Or maybe you need some time alone to figure out why you did what you did."

"Maybe," Henry agreed. "That's what you've done the past couple of years, right? How do you stand it, being alone?"

John didn't have to think about that last question. "It beats feeling like you're only good for one thing—sex."

John had had enough of being used, and with the help of his family and his medication, and a good therapist, he'd gotten past his low self-esteem and fear that no one would ever want someone with a fucked-up brain. Someone would, some day.

Chapter Two

The camping trip was a great stress reliever. There was enough physical exertion that they were both worn out, but Henry looked happy by the time they left for home on Sunday. John hoped his friend would take some time out of the dating pool and try to find some kind of way to be happy with himself. Granted, he wasn't a shrink, but it seemed to John that a lot of Henry's problems with men stemmed from his own lack of confidence. John reckoned it took an insecure person to know one, because he'd never really thought of Henry that way before. Henry laughed a lot, was outgoing and boisterous, but John could see now that it was a camouflage for Henry's doubts and insecurities.

Maybe he should get that psych degree he used to dream about.

"Come to dinner at Mom's on Wednesday, she'll be happy to see you," John told Henry when they pulled up outside Henry's house. "I'm going to tell her you'll be there, so if you don't show, she's going to hunt you down and twist your ear until you cry."

Henry shuddered. "If only you were teasing." He unbuckled then leaned over and gave John a hug. "Thanks for everything. I'll give that therapist a call."

"And Cory," John added. "You need to call him and apologize again. It wasn't enough to confess and apologize then." From what Henry had said, poor Cory had been completely astounded and deeply hurt—and angry.

"He won't ever take me back," Henry said, looking just as weary right then as he had on Friday when John had picked him up. "I fucked that up forever. I should never have told him. That whole fessing up thing just hurts the other person. I should know."

"I don't think either way of handling cheating is a good one. The best thing to do is not cheat." John held up a hand when Henry got a belligerent look on his face. "I'm not judging. I've cheated once, you know that. That's how I can say it, because I've cheated and been cheated on, too."

Henry's anger seemed to leave him deflated as he nodded. "Yeah, yeah I'd forgotten. That was back in high school, though, and it was a girl you cheated on."

"Still counts," John said. "And it was probably worse, since she caught me with another boy. I don't think catching me with another girl would have been so bad."

That same boy had cheated on him, and John had learned a lesson about faithfulness early on. He'd pretty much avoided anything serious since, then he'd taken a sabbatical from dating and fucking.

"I guess." Henry rubbed his face with his hands and grunted. He opened his door and glanced away. "You seem to be doing good. I'm glad."

"Thanks." John reached over and patted Henry's shoulder, drawing his attention back. "That's only because I have a good support network. You know me and my family will be yours, if you'll let us."

"Since my family is non-existent."

"We are your family. You know my folks love you."

Henry grinned. "And your sisters and brother tolerate me, but your nieces and nephews think I'm the shit."

John laughed at the apt description of the way his family thought of Henry. "Yeah, to all of that. See you Wednesday."

"Yeah, thanks for this weekend." Henry got out, shutting the door gently. After he'd taken his bag from the truck and gone inside, John pulled away from the curb.

They'd had a good weekend—caught lots of fish and fed lots of mosquitoes, despite spraying themselves with repellent. John vowed to be a better friend and not let so much time pass before contacting Henry again. They had cycles like that, where they'd get busy with work or, in Henry's case, a guy, then they'd need each other and it was like they'd never spent time apart. John supposed that was part of what made them such good friends. Neither one placed demands on the other.

He made it home by six and was delighted to run in to Mrs. Royal and listen to her gush about her church dinner with Mr. Marks. John would have even sworn she was glowing, and he wondered if people in love did that. His parents were usually happy to be with each other—they fought on occasion, like all couples, but even then they were respectful to each other about their disagreements. Did they glow? Maybe, John decided, on special occasions, since their love was so well-worn and grounded by roots of time, family and commitment.

His apartment seemed quiet after a weekend spent with Henry and all sorts of noisy insects. John turned on the TV to chase out the silence, not because he wanted to watch it right then. Later, after he'd taken a long shower, he might plop on the couch and veg out.

John set the shower nozzle to pulse, then turned the water on and got in the stall. He let the warm water massage the muscles in his back and shoulders as he began cleaning himself. When he reached his cock with the soapy washcloth, John saw no reason not to enjoy a luxurious hand job. He dropped the cloth and picked up the bottle of conditioner, preferring it as it didn't dry out the delicate skin on his shaft.

No rushing for work, and he wasn't so worn out from camping that he just wanted to get off and sleep. He let his mind jump from fantasy to fantasy until he found one that truly riveted him, involving a faceless man with a nice endowment. John came hard, his legs quivering as he spilled his release onto the tub floor.

Afterward, he turned the water off and got out. Drying off was done half-heartedly, and John dressed in loose sweats that barely stayed up past his ass. He imagined a lover watching him, admiring him. *It'll happen. But Mom's right, it won't happen if I stay locked up in my apartment or focus so completely on work.*

He might have passed up an opportunity here and there with one of his sales calls, but John would never engage in any kind of sexual activity with a client. That was a risk not worth taking.

It sounded so clichéd, going to church in the hopes of meeting a potential partner, not to mention kind of sacrilegious. John wasn't overly worried about that, but appearing desperate was certainly unappealing. It was like trolling the grocery store or a truck stop — except he might meet a different class of men than someone only passing through looking for a fuck.

"Won't hurt, might help, as Dad would say." John dug a pot pie out of the freezer. He put it in the microwave and was just about to pour himself a glass of milk when the doorbell rang. Since he was thirsty, and he did live alone, he took a swig from the carton then set it down before striding to the door. He wasn't expecting anyone.

"Wonder who it is," he murmured, stopping in front of the door. A check through the peephole had him frowning. In the hall outside John's place stood a short man with black hair and eyes so dark they could be black, too. He was smiling as big as that creepy striped cat in the cartoon. *Maybe I shouldn't answer. He'll go away soon if I ignore him.*

Of course, he wasn't going to do that. John called out, "Just a sec." He unfastened the chain lock, the deadbolt, and the knob lock, then opened the door. "Hi." He'd intended to say more, but the little guy was very attractive, almost breathtakingly so, and those dark eyes John had noticed through the peephole were something else. Stunning, really, framed as they were with thick lashes that curled up at the tips, and features that all in all should have had the guy on magazine covers. John was tongue-tied in the face of the handsome man.

"Hi. Um. I'm Benji Marks, Mr. Marks' grandson." He held out his hand.

John gave himself a mental kick in the buttocks and shook Benji's smaller, warm hand. "Yeah, I mean, I'm John Weston." He was an idiot!

Benji's smile, which wasn't scary at all without the peephole's distortion, stretched wider in such a way that his delight couldn't have been faked. Even his eyes lit up. "I know. Grandpa sent me up here to see if you'd be willing to give him some pointers with Mrs. Royal. He hasn't dated in years, and I think he has a crush. It's so cute!" Benji rocked up onto his toes and rubbed his hands together. "Don't you think it's cute?"

John bobbed his head, entranced by the vivacious creature chattering away at him.

"Good, so will you help? I don't know Mrs. Royal. I just moved here from Corpus, so I don't know anyone other than my Grandpa," Benji explained. "He said Mrs. Royal thought we should meet, and while we did that, maybe you could offer some tips for him to 'win her heart', as Grandpa claims." He looked up through those lashes at John and his smile turned into something sultry and teasing that had John's cock trying to stand to attention.

"She's playing matchmaker, too," John said after clearing his throat. His face felt hot, and he wished he'd have kept that realization to himself in case he was wrong. "I mean—"

Benji winked at him and tapped on the door jamb. "No, I think you're right. Can I come in?"

"Oh!" John winced and stepped back, making room for Benji to come in. "Yeah, sorry. I don't have many visitors. Just mainly family and they barge right on in."

Benji came in, his walk slow, smooth, confident. He was an attractive man, certainly. John tried not to ogle his rear end too much, but Benji's ass was one of those marvels of nature, round and plump and high on Benji's otherwise lean form. He dragged his gaze up and away, turning to shut and lock the door.

"This is a nice place," Benji said as John flipped the deadbolt. "Looks homey, you know, not like just a place to crash."

"Thanks. My family keep giving me stuff to hang on the walls or put on shelves." John looked at his tiny living room. "I had to install shelves to hold it. Really, they get the credit for the decorating. My mom and sisters can't tolerate a bare wall or unadorned surface. Walking into their homes is like walking into one of those touristy shops where there's knick-knacks all over, just waiting to either gather dust or get knocked off and broken." Crap, he was babbling. John pressed his tongue to the roof of his mouth to shut himself up.

Benji walked over to the shelf beside the window, looking at the various family photos John had placed there. He stroked a blunt finger down the biggest one, framed in silver. "Is this everyone?"

John knew what he meant and unstuck his tongue to answer. "Yeah, that's Dad, Mom, then from the left on the middle row, my sisters Stacey, Jane and Vivian. That's my brother Robert beside me on the bottom."

Benji whistled and glanced back at him. "Wow, that's a big family."

John shrugged and came a little closer to peer over Benji's shoulder at the picture. Benji watched him, and there was something in those dark eyes that made John's stomach clench. "Not really. I mean, I know the average family is supposed to be made up of two point something kids, but where that's the norm at, I haven't a clue. Most of the people I grew up with had at least two siblings, although there were exceptions, of course." He shrugged again. "Then again, what do I know? When I was kid I thought everyone was like us."

Benji went back to looking at the picture. "I don't have any brothers or sisters. In school, it seemed like another thing that made me stand out as different besides my height and being gay. I never thought a closet was anything except a place to hang my admittedly awesome clothes. Are you out?"

John didn't know what to say about the height thing. Benji *was* short. If he had to guess, John would put him at five-four, max, not that it mattered. Height had nothing to do with humanity, and Benji was first and foremost a person with feelings. He'd likely been picked on in school, and John felt a pang of sorrow for that.

"I am," he answered when he realized he'd let the silence stretch into an awkward length. "Sorry. Sometimes I just...drift off. Concentration issues." Which was the truth, if not all of it, but Benji deserved some sort of explanation. "My family's been fantastic about it." John thought back to the numerous safe-sex talks he'd gotten from his parents and siblings. "Well, maybe not fantastic, because sometimes they can be overprotective, but still, they mean well and they haven't ever tried to tell me I should be anyone other than who I am."

"You're very lucky," Benji whispered, touching another picture frame, this one of John and Henry laughing and holding up fish they'd caught. "He isn't family. Boyfriend? Or an ex?"

John moved to Benji's side and picked up the photo. "Nah, this is Henry. He's been my best friend for a long time. I just got back from a camping trip with him."

Benji cocked his head and gave him a slanted look. "He's good looking, and so are you. You're going to tell me y'all have never messed around?"

A prickle of irritation sparked in John. "I'm not going to tell you anything," he said with more snark than he'd intended, but damn it, he didn't owe Benji anything. He thought the question was incredibly rude, considering he had just met the man ten minutes ago. John stepped back and walked over to the lounge chair, where he sat down. Benji was still watching him and John fought the urge to twitch.

Benji finally sighed and looked at the picture again, then back at John. He smiled crookedly, and his tanned cheeks darkened with a blush. "Sorry. I didn't mean to be rude, it's just—" Benji waved one hand in the air, trying to convey what, God only knew. He huffed and propped his hand on his hip. "It's just that you are both so happy in the picture, and I tend to think sex makes people happy." He grinned then, an impish, sexy little curve of his lips that shot a flash-fire of want right to John's groin. "And if I was camping with you, I'd be all over you. Your personal living sleeping bag."

"It's kind of hot for one of those," John said stupidly. Benji's smile wavered and John wanted to slap himself. "I'm an idiot. I don't do this much." *Or at all, really.* That made him sound like a total loser even in his own head.

"This?" Benji asked. "Like, flirting?"

"Yeah," John muttered. "Like flirting."

Benji strolled over to him and stopped so close John could feel the heat from the man's legs on his own. "Do you just go out and get laid, then? You can't tell me you hole up here and don't do anything to get off except masturbate. You're young, attractive—" He stopped and inhaled sharply. "Are you... Do you have— Are you positive?"

John was confused for all of a second, then he was more irritated than he had been earlier. He sat up straighter and glared at Benji. "First off, what *is* it with you crossing boundaries like they don't exist? There are things people who just met don't jump into asking or talking about. I don't know you or anything and yet you've come in here and accused me of screwing around with my best friend no matter what I say, and now you're asking—"

Benji stopped him by leaning down and kissing him. It wasn't much of a kiss, because John was so startled he yelped and flung himself backwards, chest heaving as he gawped at Benji.

For his part, Benji watched him with an expression that seemed to convey a mix of confusion and amusement, maybe even exasperation. He finally shook his head and plopped down on John's couch, pulling one leg up onto the sofa to hook his arms around it as he watched John.

"What?" John squeaked out, torn between being turned on and mortified. Indignation had died down the second Benji's lips had touched his. It was amazing what one could feel in a second—soft, heat, wet—and a need that hadn't been so strong in years. John wanted to get off with Benji any way he could, and that wasn't like him. Not the improved him, at least.

Benji licked his lips and raked his gaze over John. "I just didn't think you'd be shy. You look confident. A little nervous, maybe, but that's kind of a turn-on, actually. As for me crossing boundaries, I just find being direct is the quickest route to getting what I want." He let go of his leg and lowered it so that John could easily see the bulge at Benji's groin. "I told you, I'm new here. I'm horny, and you're attractive and available, so I don't see why we can't get off together." He frowned and stared at John's groin. "Even if you're positive. I mean, I've always played safe, so it wouldn't be any different, although I have to say, I'm not sure about penetrative sex—"

John had had enough. He stood up and glared down at the presumptuous little prick on the couch. "I'm not—positive, that is—and I'm not interested, either. You're a bit too forward for me. I don't fuck around anymore. That isn't me."

Benji stood up and got in his face, or as close to it as he could reach, considering their height differences. John stood his ground as Benji stopped short of pressing up against him. The anger on Benji's face was impressive. John was surprised he wasn't annihilated on the spot from the heat of it.

"You're a judgmental asshole, that's what you are," Benji growled. "Let me guess. A reformed slut-boy who now thinks he's too good to fuck around. Saving his newly cherry ass for Mr. Right. You think you're too good for anyone else, and if I'm not proposing forever, you're not interested. Well, let me tell you—" He pointed his finger, actually brushing John's nose with the tip.

John caught his finger and held it. "Enough. You don't know me, and I don't know you. I think that'd be the best way for it to stand." He wanted to go on, to tell Benji *he* was in the wrong here, coming into John's home—a stranger, that's what Benji and John were to each other—and starting drama. John didn't feel so much like the unstable one right then. "Mr. Marks only needs to be polite to Mrs. Royal. Take her flowers, mind his manners, treat her well. Same as we should all do to one another, except maybe minus the flowers. I think you should leave now. It's been...interesting."

Benji stepped back. He rolled his eyes and huffed as he crossed his arms over his chest. "Whatever. Enjoy spending the rest of your life alone."

That resonated too much with John's fears and he had to really work to keep from responding. He had a feeling that if he did, he and Benji would just keep standing there bickering, much like the characters in a kid's book he'd read years ago. They'd stand there, stubborn and stupid, unmoving and unbending while the world went on around them.

John told himself he was better than that, and Benji probably was too. The guy obviously had issues, but so did he, and he was in no place to judge. Instead John forced himself to walk away. He went to the door, unlocked it then opened it.

Rather than stand there like some creeper, John headed for the kitchen. He was thirsty and needed to get cleaned up, but he wasn't about to strip down and get in a shower while someone who was obviously pissed off at him was there. He'd seen enough horror movies to know better.

He took a bottle of water from the fridge and opened the cap. The liquid tasted sweet and perfect on his tongue and cooled his parched throat. His stomach rumbled and he wondered what he had in the freezer — and when the hell Benji was going to leave. The man was still standing in his living room.

Finally, after John had tossed the empty bottle of water, Benji uncrossed his arms and stomped to the front door loud enough that John was sure he'd get complaints from the people in the apartment below him. "Dick," Benji snapped, then he left.

John tried to wrap his head around the bizarre encounter as he locked up the apartment and stripped for his shower. There was no making sense of it. Add his weirdness to Benji's, and the result was a nonsensical meeting that left him feeling disgusted with himself. Had he been judgmental? *Maybe a little.* Did he think he was better than the guys who went out and fucked around?

John really didn't like the answer to that. He sighed and stepped under the hot water. It wasn't that he was better than the people who screwed around. He just couldn't do the same without judging himself and plunging into a depressive state that made functioning hard if not impossible.

But he realized later, as he lay in bed staring at the utter blackness in front of him, that he used his depression as a means of keeping people away from him. Not his family, not Henry, but anyone else, anyone who might be an unknown risk, who might break his heart.

Maybe Benji wasn't totally wrong when he called me a dick. God, life is so complicated sometimes, when all we really have to do is live and die.

John closed his eyes and promised himself a good examining during his next therapy appointment. Maybe Dr. Hannah could help him figure out the mess that was his lack of sex life. Society judged a person for being sexually active, and they judged you for not having sex. John needed to figure out what *he* thought was right, because whereas he'd believed he'd known the answer to that, Benji had shaken him up and made him question his reasons for what he did and didn't do.

Chapter Three

Tuesday evening, John sat in Dr. Hannah's office and stared at his hands.

"Is there anything in particular you'd like to discuss today, John?" she asked in that soothing voice she used when he was upset.

John didn't look up as he answered, "I've had a lot on my mind, and I'm not sure if I'm okay." If his medicine was failing or if he was just in a funk.

"John, we've discussed the medicine. It isn't a cure-all."

He glanced up and she gave him an encouraging smile.

"Has something happened?" she asked.

Sighing was becoming a habit. John slid his palms over his thighs, wiping away the sweat from his skin. "Yeah, I guess. There was this incident, and it's stupid and weird, but it's bugging me. Making me question everything I've been telling myself about my personal life."

Dr. Hannah hummed and jotted something down on the pad she always took notes on. John wondered if it said something along the lines of, 'hopeless head case' or 'it's about time'. Maybe she was simply drawing squiggly lines so it looked like she was paying attention.

"I thought it was best for me to stay away from clubs, and the whole dating scene for a while," he said when he couldn't stand the silence or the way Dr. Hannah watched him expectantly. "I mean, I told you how I screwed around with everyone willing, before. I'm lucky I didn't catch something even with condom use. Nothing's fool-proof, especially with the risks I took." Rough sex, strangers, lube as an option, sucking down more cocks than he could remember. John had been out of control. He hadn't even enjoyed most of what he'd done.

"It was your way of seeking validation, and feeling wanted," Dr. Hannah murmured, repeating John's own explanations. "Yes, and I agreed that taking a step back, finding yourself and making peace with yourself, learning to love yourself was a necessary step to a better life." She wrote something else down. "And is there a problem with that now? Has it interfered with you having a social life?"

Considering John had no social life... "I suppose it is. See, here's what happened a couple of days ago." John told her about Benji and the odd confrontation that had occurred. "I still think he seriously overstepped the line more than once. It was like he had no filters, you know."

She nodded. "Hmm. Sounds like perhaps he was pushing, either to get a reaction or because he has, hmm, quirks or issues. Without meeting with him, I couldn't say, but he does sound different. Is there any chance he was perhaps high or intoxicated?"

John sat back and frowned. "I didn't even think — but he acted weird. His eyes were really dark, almost black. It could have been that his pupils were expanded instead of the iris being so dark." He tried to recall anything else that might point to Benji having been chemically enhanced. "I just don't know him, so I can't say if his behavior was normal for him." It still seemed abnormal, period.

"But he made you question your decision to remain alone for a while?" Dr. Hannah clarified.

"Yes." John swiped at a chunk of hair that flopped onto his brow. "And I think I've gotten kind of snobby about it, you know? Like I'm above all the screwing around in back rooms and alleys, and that makes me better than the people who do it. But it doesn't. I've been there and done that, and I don't like the idea of being such a stuck-up ass."

"Then don't be," she said. "That's simple enough. We are all people, all here to learn and love and, I like to believe, to help one another. Judging others may make us feel better about ourselves, but in the long run, it's detrimental because it's a cover for our own insecurities and an excuse to keep people at a distance. We hurt ourselves more than those we judge."

"Right." So he was an ass. "I guess the thing to do is to start dating again. The very idea of trying to meet people to date scares me."

"Why is that?"

John snorted and tapped his head. "Because of this. What happens when a guy I like finds out I might crash and spend six months barely functioning, getting out of bed and dragging my ass to work, then home again with no desire to do anything else?"

Dr. Hannah cocked one finely arched eyebrow at him and asked, "Well, what is it that you do now besides work?"

John was stumped for an answer at first, because he saw it then—while he wasn't in a state of depression, he was surely still in a rut as if he had been. "I went camping with Henry this weekend," he blurted out, as if that eradicated the routine he followed. "And I have dinner with my family on Wednesdays."

"Okay, that's something at least." Another note was written. "This is the same Henry who called my office yesterday and used your name as a reference, correct?"

"Yes, I guess."

She nodded. "Thank you for that. I hope to help him. However, as far as I can tell, your routine now is much the same as it was when you had your last bout of depression. Now"—she took off her glasses and steepled her fingers together beneath her chin—"I'm not advising anything wild—no clubbing and hooking up with strangers—but it might be a good idea to step out of the comfort zone you've built for yourself. There are several dating events in San Antonio, casual ways for people to meet. You've heard of speed dating, right?"

"Yeah. I don't know that it's for me," John told her.

"But you don't know that it's not," she pointed out. "For all you know, you might enjoy meeting many different men that way. All casual, no hooking up, just a few minutes to see if you might be compatible with someone else."

John didn't see how a few minutes could give him an answer to that. He thought it would take time and many conversations to be sure — but Dr. Hannah wasn't talking about being sure, she was suggesting only possibilities. John tried to keep his mind open as she listed groups and events he might be interested in.

"All of these that I've talked about, I wrote down for you." Dr. Hannah tore off a sheet from her notes. "There is no pressure, but having options might help. And, John, there's nothing wrong with you having taken the past two years to work on yourself. Someone will really appreciate that someday, when he's spending the rest of his life with you."

John blushed and took the paper from Dr. Hannah. "Thank you." He stood and said goodbye before returning to the waiting room. Once he'd taken care of his co-pay and scheduled a routine check-in appointment for a month later, John left, feeling somewhat better about everything.

He didn't have to be a judgmental prick. In fact, he didn't have to be a prick at all. That also didn't mean he had to fuck around just because he could. There was nothing wrong with valuing himself and wanting someone else to do the same.

Taco Cabana's pink building caught his eye and John drove over to the Mexican food restaurant. He didn't indulge often, because he could eat his weight in Mexican food. Today he wanted a treat, though.

The line at the drive-thru was blessedly short, and he placed his order for sweet tea, fajita tacos and sopapillas, his mouth watering as he imagined biting into the sweet treats. There were hundreds, possibly thousands, of Mexican food places in San Antonio, and some of them were just amazing. However, Taco Cabana was his favorite for fast food.

The drive home seemed longer than it was, thanks to the delicious scent of his dinner beside him. John parked and unbuckled, then he grabbed his drink and the bag of food. He got out and strode quickly across the parking lot. He paused in front of the entrance to switch the bag to his other hand so he could get the apartment lobby door when it was flung open from the inside.

"Oh!" John took a startled step back then froze as he stared at Benji. "Um." *Jesus, what do I say?* "Hi?"

Benji wasn't quite looking at him, but John was fairly certain he knew who was standing there. "Hi." Then Benji did look at him, just a quick glance that conveyed embarrassment and something else that John couldn't decipher. Benji bit his bottom lip and stepped back, still holding the door open. "Do you think I could talk to you for a minute?"

John thought of his hot sopapillas. The tacos he could warm up, but the tasty, doughy treats were best eaten fresh. He usually ate them before whatever he'd bought as a meal. Still, they were only a couple of bucks and Benji's feelings were worth more than that, even if he was prone to bursts of anger. "Yeah, okay. Come on up. I take the stairs."

Benji gave a tentative smile that seemed a bit wobbly, but he nodded and once John was inside, followed him wordlessly. John tried not to think about being in a stairwell with someone who'd been so moody and angry a couple of days prior. Benji must have known he was uncomfortable, because he was very quiet as they walked to stairs. Benji went in first, bounding up the steps.

John almost swallowed his tongue when he saw Benji's cute ass flexing and bouncing as Benji jogged up the stairs. His mouth went dry and he clenched his drink so hard the lid popped off. Benji didn't seem to hear it over his footfalls on the steps. John managed to pick up the lid without looking away from Benji's denim-clad derrière for long.

How anyone could wear jeans so tight and still move like that was beyond John. He took the stairs more slowly, losing sight of Benji at each turn of the stairwell. Benji waited for him at the exit to the third floor, panting a little.

"I'm not used to that," Benji mumbled, sweat glistening on his forehead and above his top lip.

John grunted, because he didn't really know what to say. Agreeing seemed like a way to get his head snapped off. He left the stairwell with Benji following him. John's apartment wasn't but a few yards away.

"Want me to hold something for you?" Benji offered when they stopped at number three-sixteen.

John handed him the drink then slotted the key in the lock. The awkwardness of the situation made the back of his neck itch, and he peeked at Benji. Maybe he should try being polite? "How've you been?"

Benji didn't answer and John looked fully at him. Benji's eyes really were dark brown, the pupils barely discernible from the irises. That didn't really disprove anything, because John hadn't paid enough attention to Benji's eyes on Sunday to know if his pupils had been blown.

"Can I do the whole apologizing thing inside? Please," Benji added before John could answer. "I'd like to try again."

Try what, John wanted to ask, but being the kind of dick Benji had accused him of being wasn't a very noble goal. "Sure. Come on inside, then. You can have some of my sopapillas."

"Ohhh," Benji moaned. "I love those! Did you get some of the dulce de leche dipping sauce?" He batted his long lashes at John and John decided that the man was just a flirt, and there was nothing wrong with that, he reminded himself. Some people were naturally more outgoing than he was. *A lot of people are.*

"Yeah, I did. After you." He let Benji enter first, then he followed and shut the door. "Just set my tea on the table, please. If you want a soda or water, there's some on the fridge, but I don't have any tea."

"No beer?" Benji asked, setting the tea down.

"No." John wasn't going to feel guilty for his caution about alcoholic beverages. He'd used them to escape his depression, or had tried to, too often to have them in his home.

"Huh. Okay." Benji looked at him for a second then moved over to the fridge and opened it. "I like this kind of water. It's got a sweet taste to it."

John murmured an agreement as he put the bag down and fetched some paper plates. *Might as well split dinner with him.* It wasn't going to hurt John to have half the calories he'd intended on ingesting.

"Oh, you don't have to do that." Benji stopped at the table and shook his head. "Really, especially after I was such an asshole the other day." He glanced at John. "Why would you be that nice to me?"

"Why wouldn't I?" John retorted. "It wasn't like you hit me or anything."

Benji shook his head. "That doesn't make sense to me. People can hurt you plenty without physically hitting you."

"Yeah, they can," John agreed. He sat down and pulled the tacos out of the bag, along with the hot sauce. "Are you going to stand there, or do you wanna sit?"

Benji pulled out a chair and sat down. He toyed with the edge of his paper plate—John couldn't help but see even though he was trying not to watch Benji. There was just something about the guy that caught his attention. Something other than that bubble butt he had.

"I do want to apologize," Benji began.

John gave him his full attention and Benji continued.

"I do tend to overstep, and I'm pushy and loud and obnoxious," Benji rushed out. "And it's worse when I've had a few drinks, so maybe it's best that you didn't have any beer, really. I *am* sorry for being an asshole Sunday." Benji hitched one shoulder. "I do think you're pretty hot in this controlled, 'I don't make mistakes' sort of way. Don't know that I could handle it in a relationship, but maybe we could get off together?"

It was on the tip of John's tongue to point out he hadn't mentioned being interested in a relationship with Benji, but he refrained. Partially because he didn't want to argue with the guy, and he figured that was what would happen if he did speak up. Benji's apology seemed sincere enough, but John noticed he didn't seem to be a whole lot different sober than he was drunk, if that's what Benji had been on Sunday. There was still an almost confrontational air about Benji.

"It's okay. I could have handled things better myself," John finally said. Benji seemed to relax, that combative part of him vanishing, at least in John's opinion. "Here, have some." He set half of the sopapillas on Benji's plate. Benji opened the small containers that held the dulce de leche and honey. John hoped he wouldn't bring up the part about them getting off together, because his dick had perked up when Benji had mentioned it.

What would it be like to fuck that sweet ass? No, he didn't need to know the answer to that. Didn't need to, but he wanted to.

Benji dipped a sopapilla into the creamy sauce and moaned when he took a bite of it. "Oh my God, so good," Benji said around a mouthful of the treat. He closed his eyes and moaned again. There was a dab of the sauce on his lip, and it took all of John's self-control not to lean over and lick it off. He almost whimpered when Benji licked it clean.

Benji opened his eyes just a little and looked at John. "So what do you say about getting off together? No strings, nothing but feeling good and coming until we can't move?" He leaned forward and put a hand on John's arm, squeezing the muscles there. "I know you stared at my ass when I was going up the stairs, that's why I wanted to go first. I could feel you watching me."

Would it really hurt anything? John was so hard his gut was aching. It'd been over two years since anyone other than himself had touched him in more than a friendly or familial manner.

"It's okay to say no." Benji stood and jutted his hips, the swell of his cock beneath his tight jeans unmissable. "But I don't think you want to say no. I think you want me to get on my knees and suck you until you come. That's okay, I want that, too. You don't even have to suck me back."

"Oh, God," John rasped, his sopapillas forgotten as he imagined Benji kneeling and blowing him. "Yes, please," he got out before his brain could decide anything for him.

Benji bent and brushed a sloppy, wet kiss over his lips, then he was crawling under the table. John scooted his chair back enough to give Benji some room. His hands shook and his chest was so tight with nerves he could hardly breathe as Benji got between his knees.

"Lift your butt up for me," Benji whispered, his eyes piercing John's with a hot look before he glanced away.

John was so tangled up in his body's need that he couldn't do anything but what Benji told him to. He canted his hips and Benji reached for his belt. In seconds, Benji had John's cock and balls freed.

"Nice," Benji murmured, stroking his length slowly. "Thick. I bet this would feel so good in my ass." He flicked a glance up at John then went back to watching his hands. "It's going to stretch my mouth, make me ache. I don't know if I can take it into my throat—"

John moaned then, and closed his eyes. He was going to come and embarrass the heck out of himself if Benji kept it up. The touching alone was pushing him to the edge, but add in the talking and he was in real danger of shooting off already.

John swallowed his pride as he gripped the sides of his chair. "Please," he begged. "Please, suck me."

Benji didn't torture him any longer. John's tip was engulfed in silky, wet heat that had him crying out. He wanted to watch, but couldn't keep his eyes open as pleasure spiraled through him, spreading out from his cock to every part of his body.

Benji sucked strongly on the head, and palmed John's balls in his hands. John's legs quivered and he tried to control his body, but Benji took in more of his cock, tonguing and sucking with a skill that John ever remembered experiencing.

His knuckles ached from the force of his grip on the chair, but if he let go, he feared he'd grab Benji's head and slam him down on his cock. He'd fuck his mouth and push into that tight throat, spill his load —

"Condom," John all but yelped, trying suddenly to push Benji away. He was lucky he didn't get bitten or have his balls pulled painfully. Benji let him go without resistance, and glowered at him.

"Seriously? For a blow job? I wasn't going to swallow."

John shook his head. *Benji had to know better than that — but why should he?* How many guys had John sucked off without protection? The risk might be small, but it was still there, still real. "You're worth more than that," John said, leaning until he could trace the outline of Benji's lips. He hoped the touch would soothe the anger he could see brewing in the man. "You deserve to have your lover, or whoever you're getting off with, be concerned enough to insist on keeping you safe."

"Or are you afraid I'll give you something?" Benji snarked, belligerence in his tone. "I don't even have a condom on me. It wasn't like I thought we were going to fuck. You could have just said no in the first place, I wouldn't have gone all psycho on you."

"I didn't want to say no, but now I'll have to since I don't have any rubbers either." John waited for the explosion from Benji but it didn't come. He started to put his softening dick away, but Benji scrambled to stop him.

"Wait!" Benji fisted his cock and pumped it a time or two. "No, okay? I mean, if you don't want to get off, okay, but I don't want to stop. Do you?"

John shook his head. "I told you, we need a condom for —"

"No, not that." Benji stood and freed his own cock, an impressive length for a guy of his stature. "We can do this." He straddled John's lap. "Help me." John felt for a moment like he was back in school fumbling his first hand job, but he licked his palm then took Benji's cock in hand. The heat and heft of it was beautiful, especially after so long without touching another man.

"Oh yes, just like that," Benji whispered, fisting John's length. "Damn, that feels so good."

"Yeah," John got out before biting his tongue to keep from coming. Benji was working him so perfectly it was like he knew John's cock intimately already. He thumbed the slit and John loosed a garbled sound.

"Give it up for me," Benji encouraged. "Next time, I'll bring rubbers and you can fuck my mouth or my ass, but right now, give me this."

John wanted to say there wouldn't be a next time. He didn't think Benji was what or who he needed, and Benji didn't seem to want anything more than to get off. But Benji twisted his hand around John's crown while at the same time rutting against him. John gasped and clutched Benji's cock, trying to keep a steady rhythm. His climax slammed into him the next time Benji rubbed his slit. A sound almost like a sob got past his lips, then he was coming, his body suffused with sensations that carried him to release.

Benji cursed and grunted, wiggling in his lap. John thought Benji must have come too, but he wasn't sure and his head was buzzing from the orgasm he'd just had.

"God, that was something," Benji finally mumbled, slumping against him.

"It was," John grated out. He would have to figure out just what it was later, when he could think again.

"Can we do it again sometime?"

John managed to open his eyes and found Benji peering up at him, so much hope in those dark eyes that saying no wasn't possible. He couldn't say yes, either, though, because he wanted more than this, no matter how good it had felt.

Benji must have seen something in his expression, because the hope died out in Benji's eyes, and bitterness was in his tone when he spoke. "Right. What was I thinking. You didn't even want me to blow you. I should learn, right? I should know better than to push myself on someone. I just keep doing it every fucking time. Every. Fucking. Time."

"Benji—"

"No," Benji snapped out as he got up. "I don't want to hear it. I know. You told me. Just forget it. I won't bother you again." He began swiping at his belly and cock with his shirt tail.

"Wait," John pleaded, trying to figure out how everything had gone ass over teakettle so quickly.

Benji tucked his cock back in his briefs and shook his head. "I can't do this right now. I just—" John opened his mouth to say what, he didn't know, but the glare Benji shot him had him rethinking speaking at all.

"I'm leaving. You don't want me, that's fine. I've never been enough for anyone, anyway. I'll see you around."

"Benji," John shouted, finally getting his ability to speak back. "Wait, I want to talk to you—"

Benji stopped for a moment, then muttered, "Another time, John. I need to get out of here right now."

John was left sitting with a mess on his lap and more confusion than he'd experienced in ages. He'd hold Benji to that promise of another time, though.

Chapter Four

A restless night had led to John being less than a stellar salesman at work on Wednesday. He'd muddled one potential sale completely, showing up with the wrong quotes and samples. The second meeting he'd had with a possible client had gone better, but he'd still ended up stuttering and stumbling over his words. His concentration was shot, as tended to happen when he was exhausted. John was sure he'd hear about his crappy performance tomorrow from his boss.

All John wanted to do was go home and crawl into bed. It was Wednesday, though, and he knew there was no escaping the family dinner. His mother could use guilt with a skill other moms would envy.

John shut down his work laptop and put away the loose papers. There was a place for everything on or in his desk. John preferred a tidy work area, possibly to the point of being obsessive about it. Even as tired as he was, the thought of leaving a mess — no matter how small — was unacceptable.

When he was satisfied with his area, John stood and picked up his briefcase. He waved to Dani and Jean as he left. As soon as he stepped outside, he was sweaty. John cursed and wished he'd thought to remove his suit jacket before leaving the building. At least he didn't have far to walk.

Traffic was lighter than usual, a blessing John wasn't going to question. He checked the time on the dashboard. Five-forty. If traffic kept up like it was going, he would have time to run to his place and shower.

But he might see Benji. John's stomach did an odd sort of dip and swirl thing that made him think he might need something to settle it down. Maybe he was catching a bug. He'd heard there was a stomach virus going around.

He was *not* nervous about possibly running into Benji. John tapped the steering wheel. Well, okay, he was, but only because he feared Benji would do his confusing hot and cold routine again. Jesus, John didn't need that in his life. He wanted calm, steady, dependable. Sure, that sounded a little boring, but it wouldn't be. It'd be…safe, he decided. Safe was good. Safe had saved his life, kept him from going out and taking stupid, deadly risks.

John shivered at the thought of some of the things he'd done before he'd gotten his act together. He knew he was very, very lucky not to have ended up with anything antibiotics hadn't cleared up. When he thought of the acquaintances who'd lost their lives to AIDS, drug overdoses or, too often, suicide, he couldn't quite understand how he'd been spared.

Luck, he supposed. His mother would say he'd been spared by the grace of God. If that was so, he wondered why the others hadn't been in God's good graces. It wasn't like John had bothered to believe in Him once he'd hit high school. John hadn't ever told his mom that. It'd been easier to tell her he was gay than it would be to tell her he'd given up on a God he couldn't figure out how to believe in anymore.

Thinking about religion and his loss of belief wasn't something John liked to do often. It left him feeling empty and regretful at the same time, and he wasn't sure why. Since he didn't care to deal with that now, John tried to think instead about the contracts he was working on.

The problem was, he was still nervous about running into Benji in a few minutes when he got home. Benji could be outside, or in the lobby, or the stairwell — John huffed in annoyance. He was certainly making what had happened into a big freaking deal. Benji had probably already wiped John from his thoughts, and here John was acting like he was so fabulous Benji would just have to stalk him. Yeah, his ego wasn't inflated one bit.

John parked and shut off the truck. He unbuckled and gathered his things then got out. He resolutely refused to look around, determined not to be the kind of vain idiot who thought he was irresistible. Obviously, he wasn't irresistible — he hadn't so much as even kissed another man in years up until his…whatever it was that had happened to Benji.

Well, what do you expect, living in your ivory tower — or beige apartment, like some virginal princess? John scowled at the voice in his head. There'd been a damn good reason for him to take some time out and try to make peace with himself. He wouldn't have been good for anyone, not really, if he'd kept going like he used to.

Although, come to think of it, he wasn't sure he was good for anyone now. *Look how I handled everything with Benji.*

John opened the door to the complex and let the icy-cold air conditioning blast his thoughts away. Mrs. Royal was checking her mail when he went by to check his and John stopped beside her.

"Good evening, Mrs. Royal. How've you been?" he asked, unable to just rush past her or ignore her while he checked his mail. If he was late to dinner, his mom would excuse him since he was being polite.

Mrs. Royal looked at him and waved a thin stack of mail. "Oh, it's a good evening, yes. I've been very well, thank you." He thought her cheeks pinked with a blush, but since she had on makeup, he wasn't sure. "Mr. Marks and I have been enjoying each other's company over the past few days."

John felt the first genuine smile of the day stretch his lips. "That's great, Mrs. Royal. I'm very happy for you both. If he steps out of line, though, you let me know and he and I will have a little chat." He sounded silly saying it, but he meant it. As far as he knew, Mrs. Royal had no one to look out for her.

"Oh my, you dear, dear man." She tittered and fanned herself with her mail. "Mr. Marks is a perfect gentleman. He's taking me to The Majestic tomorrow evening for the opening performance of *Showman's Spectacular*! Have you heard of it?"

"No, ma'am, I haven't."

"You work too much and play too little," Mrs. Royal told him. "Youth is gone before you know it, John. Try to slow down and enjoy it every now and then." She canted her head and had a look in her eye that set off an alarm bell in John. "Mr. Marks has a grandson, Benji, who seems like a nice young man. Perhaps the two of you could be introduced."

John didn't want to narc on Mr. Marks as the elderly man had sent Benji around to sniff out hints for courting Mrs. Royal, but he wouldn't flat-out lie for the man. There was no reason he had to let Mrs. Royal know how he and Benji had met, only that they had. John could be circumspect, though. "I've met Benji, actually. He's very" — *hot, confusing, freaking hot* — "friendly."

Mrs. Royal lit up with a smile that made her look a decade younger than she probably was. "Oh, that's wonderful! Benji's adorable, and so cute," she whispered the last two words. "I don't know what circumstances led to him living here, but I get the feeling he's been hurt in the past — but then, haven't we all?"

"Yes, I suppose." Lord, but he really didn't want to discuss Benji with anyone! John shuffled a few feet down to his mailbox and set his briefcase on the floor. "Um." He found his mailbox key and slid it in the lock, struggling to come up with something to say.

"All I received in the mail today was bills." Mrs. Royal sighed. "Oh, well, I should let you go. It's Wednesday and you have your family dinner."

John's relief at her sudden change of subject was so great that he beamed at her as he took the mail. "Yes, I do, and I better get cleaned up and to my parents' house before I get in trouble."

"We can't have that," Mrs. Royal said after chuckling. "Be careful and have a good time."

"Thank you, Mrs. Royal, you too. And let me know if I need to speak to Mr. Marks." John closed and locked the mailbox then tucked his keys in his front left pants pocket for the trip up the stairs. He gave his mail a cursory glance — bills and junk — then picked up his briefcase and took a few steps.

The elevator pinged as he neared the stairwell and it took all of John's self-control not to turn and look. It was silly to think Benji would be popping out of the elevator. There were over a hundred apartments in the building, John would guess, and he doubted every one of them was single occupancy. Add in guests coming and going, and there was no telling how many people were there. The chances of Benji being in the elevator were little to none.

Still, when he twisted slightly to open the stairwell door, his peripheral vision allowed for a better view in that direction. John saw black hair and a wide smile — Benji and Mr. Marks. It was just a glimpse, but enough of one to cause his heart to race and his head to feel a bit swoony. He couldn't handle it, so John went into the stairwell and started up toward his place.

Must be the meds. He was maybe getting resistant to them or something, and it was making him act weird. It wasn't that Benji affected him in any way, except to confuse him, John wouldn't deny that. And obviously, he'd been turned on the night before, but who wouldn't have been with Benji melting like butter all over them? The man was just so…sexually aggressive, yet giving and —

John stumbled over a step and cursed as he caught himself by slamming his briefcase against a step ahead of him. He banged his knee and his wrist ached instantly, but he didn't think he was truly injured.

"No more thinking about him while I'm walking," he scolded himself. Or while he was sitting, driving, showering —

Of course, once he was naked and in the shower, John's cock hardened, ready for his usual shower-time routine. Except this time, it didn't feel quite so much of a routine. John didn't want to jerk off, and yet he closed his eyes and images of Benji on his lap filled his head. It wasn't that he didn't want to masturbate, he simply didn't want to get hung up on Benji.

Surely one time won't hurt anything. I'll find some good porn or something this weekend to fantasize about instead, but for now… John gripped his cock with a soapy, slippery hand. He pushed the shower nozzle aside to keep the water from washing off his sudsy lube. Benji's eyes had been so hot, so full of need, he thought, as he thumbed the underside of his crown.

John had wanted to trace the thick fringe of lashes around Benji's eyes but he'd been too afraid to do such an intimate thing. Jacking each other was just a way to get off, but touching other places that wouldn't contribute to a climax was crossing a line.

Benji's lips, though—John moaned and began stroking off. God, he'd give just about anything to feel Benji blowing him without that thin layer of latex. Those pillowy lips would close around his tip, and Benji would tongue his slit. It would feel so incredible, hot and wet and tight. John moaned again and tightened his grip increasing his speed. "Yes, fuck, those lips."

John palmed his balls with the other hand and after only a roll or two, his nuts tingled with warning. John bucked his hips, imagining his cock driving in deep, Benji's throat around his tip while he sucked and sucked. The image was enough to shove him right over the edge, and John came with a grunt, his ab muscles contracting as he shot.

John stood gasping for a minute, his hand still on his softening cock. Even though he'd just come, he still felt edgy, needy. He needed to get it in gear and beat a hot path to his mom's before he was late.

It irritated him that his orgasm had left him feeling unsatisfied, and he didn't have time to contemplate the why of it. John forced himself to finish showering and to get ready. He didn't worry about styling his hair, just combed it, and since he was likely to end up wrestling with his nieces and nephews, he put on his favorite worn jeans and a soft, faded T-shirt. Flip flops completed the casual outfit, then John left, suddenly looking forward to the family meal. It'd be a distraction from his thoughts and his confusion over Benji.

Maybe his mom would even talk to him about the whole church thing again, and John would let himself be convinced to give it a try. Sometimes his stubbornness was just a show, and he needed to figure out if he was really hell-bent against giving church a shot. Or maybe he'd just use it as a dating pool, which was kind of what his mom had suggested. He snorted. Like that wouldn't be some kind of sin? Church was supposed to be for worship, or hellfire and condemnation, if you were gay.

He was ten minutes late getting to his mom and dad's, but since his mom was busy in the kitchen trying to show Jane how to make a new dessert recipe and his dad was working on Robert's car, he didn't get scolded. What he got was tackled the minute the kids came in from out back and saw him.

"Uncle John!" several of them squealed.

"Monsters!" John mock-shrieked, slapping his hands to his cheeks. "Eek!"

The familiar routine eased his mind the way nothing else had all day, and as John let the little spawns take him to the floor, he forgot to be worried or confused. It was impossible to be moody and snarky when Lacey was trying to give him a wet willy—a spit-covered finger in the ear was disgusting but hilarious to everyone except the receiver of said finger—and he was being tickled by four other kids.

John snickered and squealed when one of them, either George or Annie, tickled his armpit.

"Stop," he gasped, flailing and trying very hard not to whack a kid. They were rough and tumble little monsters, and an accidental smack wouldn't hurt them or make them cry, but John would feel like shit for it.

That wet, slimy finger he'd successfully avoided up until then went right into his ear, much to the delight of everyone but John.

"Argh! Gross!" John grabbed Lacey and tickled her ribs. "I'll get you for that, you booger!"

"I'm a booger too," little Vanessa said, trying to get to his ear.

"Oh no you don't," John growled teasingly, twisting and rolling. "Unless you want to get Lacey and make me a happy Uncle John."

Vanessa thought about it and shook her head. "Uh uh. She don't scream like you do."

"That's 'cause I'm a man," John informed her, still trying to keep from getting another wet willy. "We don't scream, either. We...we bellow, or something."

Vanessa wrinkled her pert little nose in confusion. "But you screameded. You screameded and sounded like my mommy when she sawed the mouses."

John finally got to his knees and started to stand. "I most certainly do *not* scream like your mommy." He thought about correcting Vanessa's grammar, but she was four, and he didn't have that kind of energy. He'd tease Jane later about Vanessa's claims that she'd 'sawed mouses'. There were just too many ways to interpret Vanessa's childishly adorable grammatical errors.

"No, you sounded like her," James, Vanessa's brother agreed. He was a year older than his sister and therefore thought he was very wise. "I was there."

John tipped his head up and stood. He crossed his arms over his chest. "I do not scream like a girl."

"Yeah you do," Jane called out from the kitchen. "I swear, that was like an echo from my past. I even looked for a mouse."

"Not in my kitchen," their mom scolded. "I told you to use the same exterminator we do, but did you listen? No!"

Well, he'd be off the hook for a while since Jane had just opened up a can of shoulda-kept-my-mouth-shut.

Stacey came out of the hall and started flapping her hands. "Scoot, kids, and let us visit. Go outside and play on the swing set or something."

The kids protested until she threatened them with no dessert. "Your Uncle John needs recovery time. He's getting old," she teased.

John waited until the kids were out of sight to flip her off and mouth, "Bitch."

Stacey laughed. "You know it, except you forgot the Queen in front of it. I've worked hard for that title!"

"I'm going to take it from you someday," John said, batting his lashes and cocking a hip, laying it on thick. "Everyone knows it should be mine anyway."

Stacey scowled at him. "No playing the gay card, that's not fair! You know what kind of queen I meant."

John grinned and winked at her, dropping his act. "You don't need to worry about anyone taking *that* title from you."

"Little shit," Stacey muttered, but she was snickering right along with him. "Robert could take some lessons in being fun from you. How'd we end up with such a serious older brother?"

"No idea," John told her. It was true, though. Robert was a good guy and all, but if he'd ever had a sense of humor, John hadn't seen it. "That's okay though, because Lily makes up for it. Where is she?" He hadn't seen Robert's wife outside.

"She's actually sick with some stomach bug," Stacey answered. "Mike had to work tonight, his schedule's been changed and who knows when he'll be on days again. I hate nights. So much more bad crap happens when he's patrolling on nights."

"He'll be fine, you know he will." John didn't think he would have been able to handle being married to a cop.

"He'd better be, or I'll have to smack him." Stacey took a drink of her tea and John nodded toward the back yard.

"Vivian outside pulling babysitter duty?"

"Yup," Stacey beamed. "Jane has to help with cooking, Vivian and her hubby get to babysit the herd, and I get to be lazy since I'm all knocked up again."

John's eyes were going to bug right out of his head at that bit of news. "But Chelsea's just six months old!"

She shrugged. "What can I say? Mike's a stud and I'm easy."

"Uh, you could say you had a clue about birth control," John pointed out.

That got him another shrug. "Right, because I was going to think of a condom when I woke up in the middle of the night to a naked hard—"

"Ugh, okay, okay, stop before I puke." John shuddered. He really didn't want to know the details of his siblings' sex lives. He wasn't even going to bother pointing out that Mike could have suited up and that it took two to tango. This would be Stacey's third kid, she knew how it happened. "What'd Mom and Dad say?"

"Oh, I am *so* the favorite kid right now," she replied smugly. "Yeah, you know the one kid out of five who can do no wrong? Me. The favorite. Be jealous."

John kind of was and it shamed him, though he kept all of that to himself. He wouldn't ever be rolling over groggy and horny, and impregnating his spouse. He was saved from having to make a reply by Vivian coming in the back door, a sleeping baby Bryce in her arms. She held a finger to her lips and slipped past them to put the little girl in one of the cribs in the spare room.

"I bet she gets pregnant again in the next month or two," Stacey whispered. "She always tried to compete with me. As if." Stacey fluffed her hair.

"Stop telling lies, you tramp," Vivian said. "I have no desire to swell up to the size of a damned whale ever again. I wanted to cry when I could finally see my feet after Bryce was born."

Stacey huffed and rubbed her belly. "I'll have you know, I make a very attractive whale, and being hugely pregnant helps hide the one flaw I do have, my long monkey toes. I don't mind not seeing my feet. Feet are gross."

"You and your foot phobia," Vivian said, rolling her eyes. She turned to John. "Hey, little bro, what's going on? Do I even need to ask if anything exciting happened in the past week?"

"Doubt it." Stacey frowned at him. "How come you didn't answer?"

"When did I get the chance?" he pointed out. "Y'all always ask me that same question. Am I really that boring?"

"Predictable, but there's nothing wrong with that, I guess, is there, Stace?" Vivian asked Stacey.

Stacey was studying him closely and John tried not to squirm. His sisters could have him blabbing about everything in seconds if he wasn't careful.

"It's been a rough week at work," John said, hoping to get Stacey off the scent he feared she'd pick up on. "I screwed up two sales calls today. I'm probably going to get chewed out tomorrow, and I should."

Stacey narrowed her eyes. "Huh. You don't usually screw up on the job. What's got you off focus?"

"Is it the meds?" Vivian asked. "I had to change to a completely different antidepressant after Bryce. The old one didn't do crap to help me."

John and Vivian's shared mental illness should have made them closer, he always thought, but while they got along fine and loved each other, Stacey was his closest sibling.

"I don't know. I just saw my doctor yesterday, I don't think it's the medication. Besides, you and I both know that a pill can't make everything perfect." Although it was a nice dream. All he really hoped for—and could hope for—was to be stable and not fall into the morass of dark emotions and fucked up brain chemicals. "I think I'm just having a bad week. It happens."

"Amen to that," Vivian muttered. "I had better get back outside before my loving hubby has a breakdown from watching all the kids. See ya in a few." She left them and Stacey turned a knowing look his way.

"Spill, or I'll tell Mom something's bugging you."

"Bitch is too nice of a word for you," John muttered while Stacey took his arm. "Where are we going?"

"To Mom's sewing room for some privacy."

John let himself be led along, but he had to point out the flaw in Stacey's plan. "Because Mom won't come looking for us when she realizes we're off somewhere swapping secrets?"

"I have no secrets," Stacey said, tossing her head and shaking out her brown frizzy hair. "I'm an open book. Just look at my previous attempt at honesty. You turned green. And yeah, Mom'll probably be banging on the door in five minutes, so you'd better talk fast. Does this involve sex? Did you get laid?"

John groaned and covered his face with his hands as she pushed him into the room. "Stace, come on," he whined.

She whooped, albeit not as loud as she normally did, and he could hear her doing a pitter-patter dance. "All right! It's about time, bro. I was afraid you'd turn into some serious, bitter prude."

John glared out at her from between his fingers. "Harsh, Stace." That 'bitter' part, especially. "And there wasn't any, you know…"

She cocked her head and blinked, obviously willing to wait until he actually said it.

Fine then, but if I die from embarrassment, she's going to feel bad. "We didn't have anal sex. It was just hands."

How Stacey understood him, when he'd blurted it all out together until it sounded like one indecipherable mess, was beyond him. But she got enough of it, because she made an obscene and very familiar gesture with one hand.

"Just this?"

"Don't *do* that!" John yelped, then amended, "except maybe you should do that after you have this baby and you wake up with a horny husband in bed with you."

"I'll keep that in mind, although you gotta admit, it isn't the same as —"

"Stop it," John pleaded. "I can't tell you what happened if I'm wigging out from your oversharing."

"Fine," Stacey huffed. "But you don't get to leave out the good parts, even if it was just hand jobs."

Lord, he was just never going to have any kind of sex again. John started talking.

Chapter Five

"Josie's daughter Francine said it's a homosexual church."

John swallowed his mashed potatoes and wished his mom wouldn't push him on this while everyone was there. It felt too personal, but then again, his family had always been close.

"I've never heard of a homosexual church," Robert said.

John glanced at him, trying to figure out if his brother had made one of his very rare jokes. Dry humor didn't even begin to describe it.

"Yeah, so it's like, gay?"

John's mom pointed her fork at Vivian. "Don't be smart. I can throw this pointy utensil and wing you. You too, Robert. You all know what I meant."

"It's a church serving the LGBTQ community," Jane clarified.

Mom pointed the fork at her. "I said that already." She looked at John. "So it wouldn't be like those churches that are preaching hate. It'd be maybe like our church, but with available men for you."

"Mom!" John hunched over while almost everyone else laughed.

"What? I want all my kids to have good spouses. You've been alone too long, and you need someone who'll love you like your dad and I love each other."

John wasn't sure that existed for him.

"Your mom's just trying to help," his dad said, patting his back. "And it wouldn't hurt you to step foot in a church, even if it isn't that one. The Lord's been good to us. Thanking Him occasionally might be smart."

Right on cue, Lacey started a horribly off-key version of *Amazing Grace.*

"No singing at the table," his mom told her. "I am *not* the pushover kind of grandma."

"Which means she'll have you scrubbing toilets if you keep it up," Vivian told her niece. "Trust me, I know this for a fact."

Lacey had stopped singing and she asked Vivian, "You got in trouble too?"

Vivian gave her a look of mock-horror. "Me?" She put a hand over her heart. "Nevah. I was the best kid ever in existence. Now your mom and Aunt Stacey, oh boy. They were always in trouble. The stories I could tell…"

John was grateful to his sisters for taking him out of the line of fire. His family could be nosy and annoying, but mostly they were wonderful and he loved them. The rest of dinner passed with more bickering and teasing, and scolding on occasion. After everyone had eaten, John helped to clear the table. He started rinsing dishes but his mother came over and tapped his hand.

"No, you don't need to do this."

They had this argument regularly. Once a week, in fact.

"Yes I do, Mom. There's a crapload of dishes from feeding all of us, and I'm not leaving them for you to do. Stace or someone else can help me." Usually it was Stacey, but since she was crowing about being the good kid...

"I'll help. I haven't had time alone to talk with John in a while."

John glanced at Robert who'd stepped beside him. "Seriously?"

"Why not?" Robert replied.

"This is a good idea, you two boys having brother time. I like this." Their mom kissed them both then left.

"This is weird, is what it is," John said. He stuck his tongue out at Robert.

Robert merely started on the stack of dishes. "Scoot down. You can stick 'em in the dishwasher."

"If Mom would let us get her a new one, we wouldn't have to wash the dishes first."

"Then we wouldn't have time for you to tell me what's bugging you." Robert handed him a plate.

John scowled and rinsed it. "What is it with everyone asking me that?"

"I know you and Stacey were off talking, and that happens when one of you aren't happy about something. She's flying high on getting knocked up again, so that means you got a problem." Robert shrugged. "Easy enough to figure out. If Dad hadn't sent me in to dig in the hall closet for his rags, I wouldn't have heard y'all and you'd be off scot-free from this inquisition."

"Inquisition? Are you going to torture me?"

Robert held up the sink's spray nozzle. "Waterboarding. It can happen anywhere."

"That's two," John muttered.

"Two what?"

"Jokes in one night from you."

Robert grimaced and went back to washing. "I know I'm not the funniest person in the world, but I do have a sense of humor. And I wasn't joking about the church. I was pointing out the improper sentence structure or whatever."

"O-ookay."

"But the waterboarding, yeah, that one was a joke. Kind of." Robert handed him another plate—and squirted him with the spray nozzle.

"Hey! What the fu-fudge," John snapped, barely catching himself before saying a word he'd swear his mom could hear from anywhere in the house.

Robert grinned and gestured at him with the nozzle. "Heh. Look at that. It's kind of shaped like Africa."

"This is just too much weirdness in one night for me." John scowled at Robert then yanked the nozzle out of his hand. "Give me this."

"If you squirt me—"

"I won't. Moron." John didn't want to end up having to mop the kitchen floor, which was what would happen if they got into a water fight. Besides, he'd get Robert back another way. "We were talking about hand jobs," he said in a nasty tone.

Robert just shrugged. "Okay, like I've never had one. What?" he asked when John gawped at him. Robert shook his head. "Seriously, John, women jerk guys off, too."

"I know that." Of course he did. His brain had just shot to his idea of a hand job, which did not involve women in any way. "I just can't believe we're having this discussion."

"But you brought that part of it up," Robert pointed out. "I just want to know what's bugging you."

John wanted to ask why he cared, but that would have been hateful and unfair. Robert had been the one to confront him one night after John had gotten in a mess and had needed help. He'd accidentally called Robert, and when Robert had found him — well... John had ended up having a surprise intervention.

"I guess I'm just restless, but...but scared to change anything, you know?" He glanced at Robert, who nodded. "It's been a couple of years, and I'm doing so much better. I mean, I still have bad days, but who doesn't? I'm just, I guess I'm afraid if I change anything, I'll end up like I used to be."

"Huh. I don't think that'd happen unless you make bad changes. You planning on making bad choices?"

"No," John scoffed. "But I just started thinking about maybe trying to meet a decent guy, and the next thing I know..."

John found himself explaining what had happened between him and Benji for the second time that night. Robert's face turned a reddish-purple when John mentioned the sex part, but he put that down to Robert not particularly wanting to hear the dirty details about his little brother's sex life. With more than a decade between them, Robert and he had never been super close, but John was beginning to think that might be changing when Robert nodded once he'd stopped talking.

Robert put an arm around his shoulders and gave him a squeeze. "Look, I don't know the guy, of course, but it seems like Benji's got you tied in knots. Maybe it's because there is something between y'all. Maybe it's just lust since you haven't gotten laid in years. Maybe it's more. I sure can't tell you, but my advice is, get out. Either go to this meat-market church Mom keeps trying to shove down your throat, or find an organization like...like San Antonio Gay Rights Association or something, and see if you can help people and help yourself."

"How do you know there's a San Antonio Gay Rights Association?"

"I just made that one up," Robert admitted. "But come on, there's got to be some places like it here. Have you ever looked?"

"No, but actually, Dr. Hannah gave me a list of places that might—" John laughed. "Aw, God, it's like a community effort to get me laid or something."

Robert let go of him and swatted John's hip. "No, it's to get you the perfect man, not get you laid. We all love you and want you to be happy."

"Do I hear brotherly bonding going on?" Stacey said, walking into the kitchen. "Y'all cut it out. Robert, you can't be John's favorite. I won't give up my spot."

"Wouldn't dream of it." Robert tipped his head at John. "Call me if you need me. Lily and I are going to Tahoe for our anniversary in three weeks, we'll be gone for the weekend, but other than that, I'm here for ya."

"Everyone's here for me apparently," John said after Robert went into the other room.

Stacey grinned. "Ain't it great?"

It kind of was, John decided. He felt strangely relieved, as if just talking about Benji had removed pressure John hadn't realized he'd had on him. There was no reason he had to hide from Benji, and no reason he had to even talk to the guy. All he had to do was live and try to be a good person. Hopefully, he'd meet someone who was looking for a steady, long-term relationship.

* * * *

John didn't see Benji when he got home. The stairs were empty, as was the lobby. In the hallway, as he unlocked his door, he could hear a TV on somewhere, but that was it. No surprise ninja-Benji attack.

A second shower helped him relax enough that John sprawled on his bed and went to sleep instantly. He never slept a solid eight hours, always waking two or three times at night, sometimes more. As long as he fell back to sleep easily, he was fine come morning.

The alarm went off and he swatted at it, then stretched and yawned. He did a quick scan of his emotions and decided he was in an okay mood. In the bathroom, he was glad to see the slight bags he'd had under his eyes yesterday were almost gone. He touched one and frowned, wondering if he should invest in some skin cream or something. He wasn't even thirty yet. Should he be worried?

No, he had just had a bad night's sleep the night before. He'd be fine. Besides, Stacey and the other sibs would tease him mercilessly if they found out he was trying to pretty himself up—and they would find out, somehow. It was the kind of karma he had.

John went through his usual morning routine, taking his time as he always got up two hours before he had to be at work. Breakfast was scrambled eggs and toast with a dollop of hot sauce, plus coffee, and more coffee. He brushed his teeth and made sure he didn't have food on his chin or shirt, then he deemed himself ready to leave.

And stopped short when he saw a piece of paper in front of the door, in the way that meant someone had to have slid the note under it.

John's stomach dipped and he immediately thought of Benji. There was no one else who'd possibly leave him a note. Mrs. Royal was about the only other person he really talked to there, and she'd just knock on his door.

He'd done so well, not thinking about Benji at all that morning. John sighed and looked at the note from where he stood. It was written on some creamy off-white paper rather than notebook paper. Was that supposed to make him feel special?

The note might not be from Benji. It could be a flyer, or an angry message from a neighbor who had a complaint, or, or... *Stop being an idiot*, John told himself. He walked over and squatted, reaching for the note.

The paper *was* smooth, soft, and he'd swear he smelled a hint of cologne other than his own. John lifted the note to his nose and sniffed. The familiar scent shot right to his balls. *Benji. Damn it, why does he have any effect on me at all?*

John stood and unfolded the note. The message was short.

Twice I've been an ass. I'm sorry. Benji.

"What does this mean, even?" John stared at the note. He got that it was an apology, but the why of it and what happened next confused him. "There's nothing else—" John turned the paper over, scrutinizing it for any mark at all and not finding a damned thing. "Shit."

Did this mean Benji wanted something more from him? John didn't think so. He was making a big deal out of nothing. Benji just wanted to apologize for being butt-hurt because John had been, well, he'd been an asshole. He could have said something instead of staring at Benji like he had sprouted another eyeball.

Even though Benji had been pushing, John understood why. There was a connection between them, and it was probably only sexual—they were young, unattached, and horny, and Benji was un-freaking-believably hot. Benji just wanted to know if they could get off again together and John had gone all uptight, virginal prude on him. It wasn't like Benji had asked about forever. All John had needed to do was talk about it with Benji, make sure they were both on the same page. Fucking, getting off together, but if John found someone he could have more with, Benji and he would part. Same for Benji, though it hadn't sounded like Benji was interested in anything but busting a nut.

And John was a judgmental bastard, wasn't he, for thinking he was above just enjoying that kind of release with another man.

Or was he just making excuses to do it again?

"God damn, I need more coffee to figure this shit out." John looked back longingly at the empty pot. Then he saw the time on the kitchen clock and cursed again.

"Talking to myself, swooning over a piece of paper." He kept muttering as he gathered his things and left for work. By the time he reached the first floor, he'd gotten his head on better. He'd work hard today and make up for the contract he'd completely bungled yesterday. There were new sales leads, and one of the designers from the Jassic Hotels line had said he'd call Thursday—

John's entire body flashed warm when he saw Benji in the lobby with Mr. Marks. Benji didn't see him at first, so John had a moment to appreciate how attractive Benji was all over again. He was dressed in a dark pair of jeans so tight John could probably have felt every vein on Benji's dick through them. A form-fitting dark blue T-shirt accentuated his muscled body. Benji laughed at something his grandfather said, and the sound of his laughter caused fluttery sensations in John's belly.

He was drawn to Benji sexually, there was no denying that. But he didn't know anything about the man. He didn't even know what Benji did for a living. All he knew was the way Benji's lips tasted, the look on his face when he needed, when he came, the sounds he made—

John stopped himself before his dick made a mess of his pants. He didn't have time to go back upstairs and put on clean ones if he ended up with a damp spot on the front of the ones he had on. Rather than approach Benji, John continued to hang back, unsure of what to do. Did he go up, say hi, or would that be awkward? He could sell carpeting to almost anyone, but one on one human interactions were just tricky.

For all he knew, Benji might not want him around. The apology didn't say, 'Let's do it again'. In fact, it might have been Benji's way of blowing him off for good.

Or, Benji might have told Mr. Marks that John was a giant asshole, and wouldn't that make for a fun time. John had visions of getting chewed out by the elderly man.

But, it could be that Benji wanted to be friends, with or without benefits. John needed to stop cowering like a, well, like a coward, he supposed, and head for the door. Whatever would happen, would happen.

Except Benji turned his head then, and spotted John. It must have been obvious to him somehow that John had been deliberately hanging back—perhaps because he was still holding the stairwell door open.

The look on Benji's face, a split-second of that warm bubbly happiness, was instantly replaced with a hurt expression that he hid by turning his back to John.

Well shit. I've done it again. He'd let his insecurities and social ineptness get in the way of his being a decent human being. John let go of the door, the sound of it closing unmistakable. Benji didn't look back, though, steering his grandfather to the doors leading outside.

John let them go. If he was late to work, so be it. That hurt look Benji had sent him was going to bother him until he straightened things out with the man, but running after him now would be foolish. At least, that's what John kept telling himself.

He *was* late getting to work, and he *did* indeed get an ass-chewing from his boss. After sincerely apologizing and promising to get his head out of his rump, John went back to his desk and rested his head in his hands. He wasn't as strong or as healed as he'd thought he was if something like what had happened with Benji was tearing him up so much.

It was the confusion that was the worst. There was only one way to clear that up. He'd talk to Benji tonight.

Having made the decision, John began to feel better immediately. It was the right thing to do. Maybe he would even take Benji up on the no-strings-attached fling, as long as they were both truly okay with it. He'd need to make sure Benji knew he was looking for more, though. It was too bad Benji had said he wasn't interested in anything long term, John mused, finally admitting what was at the root of the problem for him. And that meant he probably shouldn't get into a casual fuckbuddies things with Benji. John was afraid he'd end up hurt when Benji found someone else to have sex with. Still, they would talk, or he'd talk and try to apologize if Benji would listen.

He worked a deal with Jassic Hotels to create a pretty, durable design for their two new hotels going up south of San Antonio, where there was a dearth of housing and rooms for the oil workers flooding the area. Durable was exceedingly important, considering the grit and grime that would be tracked across the carpets. John could back up their product's claims with proof from other hotels they'd carpeted in the same areas.

By the end of the day, he was in a much better mood, but he was nervous, too. Excited at the possibility of talking to Benji if they could get past the weirdness that had happened between them. John tried not to think about touching Benji, feeling him writhe and come in his arms. That was a direction he wasn't sure was wise for him, but it wasn't off the table should Benji want to talk about it. John mused over the possibilities as he drove home.

He ended up having to park farther from the apartment building than usual but it wasn't a big deal. He strode through the parking lot, looked for Mr. Marks' vehicle and found it. Beside it was a little hybrid car that probably got great mileage and was a nightmare to ride in.

John would be terrified to drive a little car in San Antonio, and definitely in the towns farther south where oil trucks and eighteen-wheelers owned the roads. The traffic fatalities in those areas had skyrocketed since the Eagle Ford Shale find, or at least the wrecks were getting a lot more attention now. It seemed like there was one on the news every day now.

When he saw the license plate frame from a dealer in Corpus Christi, John was certain the car belonged to Benji.

John didn't see Mrs. Royal or anyone else he knew when he went inside. At the mailboxes, everyone was a stranger to him. One man, older and attractive with white streaks in his dark hair, might have been eying him up. John wasn't sure that was the case, but he tried a little smile, hoping he wasn't coming off like a total dork.

The gentleman smiled back and there was a definite spark in his blue eyes when he approached John.

John wondered how it was he'd suddenly become a man magnet.

"Hello. I'm Shane Ellis."

John shook Shane's hand. "John Weston." Shane's grip was firm but not annoyingly so. He told himself to be cool, calm, and avoid being an idiot. "At the risk of sounding like I'm using a bad pick-up line, which I'm not, I've never seen you here before."

Shane released his hand, brushing John's palm with his fingers. "I'm new here, sort of, if you can still consider a couple of months new. Usually I work supervising the second shift at the flour production plant, so I check my mail in the mornings. Looks like getting a promotion has more perks than I'd thought."

"You just got promoted?" John didn't know what management levels there were at the flour mills. He'd never really given it any thought, though he saw the tall mill building every day that he worked.

"I did," Shane said, smiling even wider, "and my schedule changed to days, so I'm a little thrown off, still trying to adjust. Would you...would you like to maybe get some coffee one evening after work? There's the Starbucks down the street."

John couldn't quite mask his surprise. He must have done something different to be hit on twice in one week.

"I didn't mean to—" Shane said, his smile fading.

John realized he'd been quiet too long and quickly started talking. "No, no, I'd love to, seriously. I'm just—" He huffed and ran a hand through his hair. "Well, it's fair to say I'm not the best at stuff like this."

"Talking?"

"Talking to attractive men," John clarified, earning him another smile. "Put me at work, and I can be pretty coherent, but this kind of thing, I'm out of practice with."

Shane's smile reached all the way to his eyes, setting the color off and framing it with fine lines around the outer edges. "Oh, I don't know. I think you're doing quite well. I'm flattered, and looking forward to meeting you one evening, soon."

It was just for coffee, and wasn't really a date. John saw no harm in it. "Tomorrow, although Friday might be a mess at Starbucks, everyone wanting some caffeine before hitting the clubs."

"I'll risk it if you will," Shane told him. "Six-thirty?"

"Okay. And, um, I'm in three-one-six if you need to cancel."

Shane nodded. "Saw it on the box. I'm in one-one-two. Have a good evening, John. It's been a pleasure meeting you, and I look forward to tomorrow evening." They shook hands again and John wished he'd felt some of the same attraction for Shane that he felt for Benji. Maybe it would happen, eventually, if he and Shane were compatible.

He watched Shane walk away and while the man was fit and had a butt that should have made John's mouth water, there was no visceral tug of lust or anything really, more than just the hope that coffee with him didn't end in disaster.

In the stairwell, John heard the faint patter of footsteps ahead of him. He didn't rush, not wanting to have to be friendly when he was trying to figure out why he wasn't wanting to fuck Shane into the mattress. The man was every bit as handsome as Benji. Bigger, more refined looking, but hot enough to make the Texas heat seem chilly.

And yet I don't want him. Maybe that just means Shane and I could have a more stable relationship, none of the hot and cold — Oh, what the hell am I doing? Planning our lives out?

John hit the bar on the exit door leading to his hallway, irritated with himself. He was acting like a desperate fool, and probably exuding some kind of desperate fool pheromone that was drawing the men to him.

The idea of it made him giggle before he clamped his lips down tight over the sound. Giggling wasn't something a man did, not in Texas. There were exceptions, but John had worked hard to ditch that one trait. He worked with decent people mainly, but there were the usual homophobes that lived in a state run by a homophobic governor. Some of them were clients, and if they thought for a minute that he was gay, a contract might not be all he lost. He knew too well what could happen when some bigot decided to play his version of God.

John's mood was every bit as messy as it had been when he'd left that morning. He unlocked his apartment then went inside, automatically looking on the floor, holding his breath, hopeful — only to find nothing unusual there. Just the same beige carpet as always.

John reached the front left pocket of his slacks and pulled out Benji's note. Just touching it made him feel better than touching Shane had. It was ridiculous. He needed to get his act together and stop thinking with his dick. That method had only ended up with him feeling like a complete useless slut before. This time, he was going to use his head.

His heart would just have to follow along.

Chapter Six

Finding Benji hadn't panned out on Thursday night. No one had answered at Mr. Marks' place. John slept badly, which was why he told himself he didn't resist the impulse to go look at the floor in front of the door.

Jesus, he was pathetic, John thought when he saw nothing but carpet. What was he, back in elementary school, waiting for a note asking 'do you like me too?'

He showered and skipped the shaving. One day's worth of stubble should be allowed on casual Friday. He put on a nice pair of jeans and a long-sleeved, green, button-up Oxford over a white tank top. He left the top button undone on the outer shirt, and put a nice tie in his briefcase. Then he slid on his brown leather belt and his hiking boots, and he was ready to go.

There was still no note.

John decided breakfast was too much trouble and he left his apartment, scowling, angry for no good reason. He took the stairs at a jog, hoping to wear off some of his pissy mood. If he was still this way by the time he got off work, he'd make a pleasant coffee companion for Shane — *not*. It'd be too late to cancel by then, and he didn't want to cancel anyway.

John came out of the stairwell, and for the second day in a row, he froze, not letting the door shut behind him, holding onto it with his fingertips. He didn't think he could have moved if he'd tried, not when all he could do was stare at Benji, who was talking to another man. Their heads were close together, and there was an intimacy there that John might have been imagining.

Or not. The man framed Benji's jaw with one hand and tipped his head up, then right there where anyone could see — where John could see, damn it — the guy kissed Benji. It wasn't a sloppy, tongue-fucking-mouth kiss. No, as John watched, his chest aching for some weird reason, Benji was kissed tenderly, lovingly, as if he meant something true to the guy.

John turned away and stepped back into the stairwell, closing the door softly. He stood there, heart thundering like it was stampeding in his chest. No wonder he hadn't been able to find Benji last night. He'd been busy, and here John had felt bad, had thought he'd hurt Benji.

Jesus, he was stupid. Stupid, gullible, and full of himself for having thought he'd meant anything to Benji. He must have misread Benji's expression yesterday. He sure didn't look hurt today.

After ten minutes, John figured Benji and his — whatever the guy was — had to be gone. They couldn't stand there making out, that was for sure. He pushed the door open again and almost hit Benji with it.

Benji startled and yelped, slapping a hand to his chest. John gripped the handle of his briefcase so hard his fingers ached. "Sorry," he got out. Nothing else good was going to make it past his lips, so John turned and headed for the doors to the parking lot.

"John—" Benji called, and the sounds of his footsteps followed.

"I'm late," John bit out. He would *not* say anything snarky. He wouldn't. He couldn't, because all he could think about was how Benji wanted to get off with him, nothing more, and the way that guy had kissed Benji, which sure wasn't anything like friends who'd just had a little fun.

That kiss had been...sweet, and that was worse. Worse, because John didn't know why Benji had bothered getting off with him when he had someone like that who cared about him.

"John, please, I just—"

Benji grabbed his arm and John shook him off, barely able to restrain himself from snarling or throwing a punch.

And that person *was not him*. John hadn't ever been deliberately mean or violent. Not when he'd been sober, at least.

"Leave me alone, Benji." That was the best he could do, and he still couldn't look at the man.

"Oh, very mature. I just wanted to talk to you about—"

"You're calling me immature?" John snapped, finally looking at Benji. Geez, why'd he have to be so cute? "When you're slipping notes under my door and making out with some guy in the freakin' lobby?"

Benji jerked back, his eyes going wide and his tanned skin paling. There was a suspicious shimmer to his eyes that John forced himself to ignore as he turned away. Whatever Benji had to say, John didn't want to hear it.

* * * *

He didn't remember the drive to work. Not wanting a repeat of the other day, he poured himself into his job. On the occasions where he thought about Benji, he told himself he was being a complete fool and had been ever since he'd met Benji. They didn't know each other, they'd just beat each other off once. John had done a hell of a lot more with many guys, and had never considered himself hung up on any of those men.

He took a working lunch, and while he was eating his meatball sub, John had an insight about the whole mess. It was going without sex for so long—that was what had made him some freakishly clingy weirdo. John would rectify that. He had a date for coffee with Shane, and if that led to more, well, then he'd go with it.

With his luck, he'd become a Shane-leech next. John snorted and managed to suck food down the wrong way at the same time.

"Jesus, John, are you okay?" Paul said, thumping him on the back while John coughed and spluttered. "What'd you do, try to inhale a meatball?"

John gasped and somehow got air into his lungs. He leaned over to escape the pounding on his back and grabbed his drink. Thankfully, Paul didn't keep up with the pseudo-help. John took a drink, barely kept from hacking again, then wiped at his eyes after he swallowed.

"Seriously, are you okay? I thought you were going to keel over."

"I'm fine, Paul." He swallowed, because that squeaky voice was not going to work for him. "Just can't eat and think at the same time, apparently."

Paul chortled and pushed a lank strand of hair off his forehead. "Yeah, well my wife would say it's a guy thing."

If he only knew how true that was. John shot Paul a grin. "Wouldn't argue with your wife, dude. I learnt from watching my mom and dad, she always won."

"No kidding. Macy can argue circles around me. I forget what we were arguing about in the first place, then she's got me." Paul nodded. "She's the best."

John agreed with him and went back to trying not to die by meatball inhalation. The rest of the day was uneventful, and he managed to keep his focus on work. Come Monday, he'd have a busy day calling on potential customers.

Friday traffic was almost always awful, and today was no exception. John didn't even bother going to his place first, because it was six-fifteen when he pulled into the Starbucks parking lot. He got the last spot available and checked his appearance in the rear-view mirror before he shut the truck off. *Relax. Look like you're going to have fun, not like you've wanted to punch something…someone, most of the day.*

John closed his eyes and used the relaxation techniques he'd learned. Why he hadn't thought of them sooner—well, castigating himself now wouldn't help. John took several deep breaths, exhaling slowly in between. Once he felt calm and in as good of a place as he could get, John unbuckled and got out. He shut the door and locked the truck then made his way into Starbucks.

The place was crowded, no surprise, but Shane was already there, sitting at a table right up front.

"Hey," John said, coming over and standing by the table. "Mind if I have a seat?"

"Sure. It's good to see you."

The way Shane's expression lit up did wonders for John's ego, although he thought maybe that didn't need any stroking after the whole Benji debacle. Then again, he could be wrong.

"Good to see you too," John said as he sat across from Shane. "Glad it's Friday?"

"Oh yeah." Shane leaned back a little and looked John over. "I love my job, don't get me wrong, but knowing that I might have a date with a handsome man afterwards sure made the workday drag." Shane raised an eyebrow. "This is a date, right? I didn't read you wrong?"

John had kind of been surprised to hear Shane call it a date, even though he'd hoped it would be. "Yeah, yeah it is. I wasn't sure what you were thinking, you know, if it was just coffee or if there was maybe something more you were looking for."

Shane gave him a sultry look and John thought they might be skipping the get to know you part. John wasn't quite ready for that.

"So, you want another coffee?" John nodded at Shane's cup. "I could use some myself, and maybe a piece of lemon pound cake. God, that stuff is *so* good."

Shane blinked and seemed to almost shake himself, his head moving slightly. "Yeah, okay. That'd be good. Here" — he shifted, raising up on one hip.

"Nah, it's good, I've got it," John told him. "What are you drinking?"

"Uh, just coffee, but I wouldn't mind switching it up and getting one of those caramel frothy things, if that's okay."

"Sure. Be right back." John got up and got in line. The baristas were quick and efficient, and despite the long line, it only took John fifteen minutes to get their drinks and the cake. "Have you had the lemon pound cake before?" he asked as he handed one slice of it over to Shane.

"No, but it smells divine." Shane took it and moaned a little when he bit into it. "Oh my God. How have I lived without this?"

"Add this too and you have a mouthgasm in the making." John set the caramel coffee drink in front of Shane.

"Mouthgasm?" Shane said after he'd swallowed.

John felt his cheeks heating but he met Shane's hot gaze. "Yeah. Like an orgasm in your mouth that you can taste."

He'd decided, while in line, that if Shane just wanted to get laid, then fine, that's what would happen. There wasn't the same tug of lust that John had felt for Benji, but considering where that had taken him, why would he want to feel it again?

Shane cleared his throat and stirred his coffee, not looking at him. "Excuse me, I'm not trying to be an ass, but—"

He finally looked at Shane.

"I thought you weren't that into me, to quote someone, somewhere. Sort of."

John couldn't help it, he chuckled. "I'm really not good with this stuff, kinda been out of the game for a couple of years."

"Now, why would a young, good lookin' guy like you be out of practice?" Shane licked his lips, catching a dab of whipped cream. "You don't have to tell me if it's too personal. We don't really know each other, and honestly, while I'm sure you're a great guy with lots of interesting things to talk about, I'd really just like to take you back to my place." Shane leaned closer as desire began to bloom in John. "I want to suck you dry, John. Is that too personal for you?"

John had a flash of other lips, parting— *No. No, I won't go there. Shane's handsome, willing, and I'm tired of stressing out over everything to do with sex.* "No," he rasped out. "No, it isn't."

Shane stood up, taking his cake and coffee. "Then, if you'd care to give me a ride? I walked, figured it'd do me good to stretch my legs."

Oh, there was a glint in Shane's eyes that finally had John's cock at full mast.

"Yeah, no problem." John tugged his shirt tails out of his pants and stood, gaze locked with Shane's. "Let's go."

They left Starbucks and didn't speak as they walked to the truck. John unlocked the doors and got in.

"You're sure about this?" Shane asked. "I won't be mad if you don't want to."

John shot him a smile. "I'm a little nervous, that's all. I don't do things like this anymore, and I don't—you know, I'm just nervous." He'd almost said he didn't want to go back to being the guy who fucked everything, but common sense had kicked in and stopped him.

"We don't have to do anything, although I won't lie. I've wanted to suck your dick since I saw you. I'm not big on anal, though, so if that's a deal breaker for you..." Shane trailed off, watching him.

John wondered if he'd ever been so knowledgeable about his own wants. He'd fucked and sucked and occasionally bottomed indiscriminately for a while before getting his shit together. During all that sexual debauchery, he'd gone along with whatever whoever he was with had wanted. He hadn't cared, as long as he'd got off.

"Blow jobs are fine," he said, and actually felt relieved. "But, uh, I have to insist on condoms."

Shane nodded. "No problem. I always play safe."

"Do you play a lot?" John couldn't help but ask as he pulled out of the parking lot.

Shane shrugged. "Not a lot, but occasionally. I had someone once, but…"

John looked at him and he shook his head, seeming to age right before John's eyes.

"Anyway, he's gone. I can't imagine loving anyone like that again, so I guess if that's an issue, too—"

"We're good," John interrupted. "I want to be with someone who wants me long-term, sure, but I've come to realize hiding away and denying my needs isn't helping me any. It's just making me a socially awkward horn-dog."

Shane laughed and it did wonders for him, changing his entire expression from a lonely, heart-broken man to someone who was ready to let go for a while.

It only took a few minutes to get to the apartments, and John followed Shane to his door. "I usually take the steps up three flights, seems strange to go to a door on the first floor."

Shane winked at him. "Now I know how you got that amazing ass. I might not like to…you know, but I can still admire a piece of art." Shane unlocked his door.

John didn't know what to say to that other than 'thank you', so that's what he did. John was getting a little nervous, though he tried not to show it.

"You can still say no," Shane told him. "No harm and all that."

Shane's consideration just made John more determined to go through with their plans. "I'm good. I don't want to mess it up, but giving head's gotta be like riding a bike, right?"

"You don't have anything to worry about, John," Shane said as they stepped into his place. Shane shut and locked the door, then turned to him with an expression of need that hardened John's cock, as it had begun to flag.

"I told you, I want to suck you off." Shane grabbed his hips and spun him, putting John's back to the door. "You don't have to do anything. In fact, I'd prefer it if you just let me handle everything."

Control, that's what gets him off. It wasn't something John could handle on anything close to a regular basis, but for tonight, he was okay with it. "Okay."

Shane smiled and John thought he was going to get a kiss, but no, Shane merely began sliding down his body.

"God," John sighed as Shane mouthed over his erection. Through the denim and his boxers, he could still feel the heat and moisture from Shane's mouth. He started to rest a hand on Shane's shoulder but Shane caught his wrist, took his other one, too, and pressed his palms to the door.

Got it. John curled his fingers against the door. Shane went back to driving him crazy, scraping his teeth over John's shaft and working John's belt buckle free.

John began to pant, watching, waiting. Shane took his time, slowly unzipping John's pants, licking the outline of his cock, stimulating him to the point where John almost forgot his requirement regarding the condom.

Shane didn't, though. He took one out of his own pocket, smiling almost shyly. "I was hoping. I'm not everyone's cup of tea, with the rules I have, but—" He ran his finger down John's dick from slit to base.

"Fine, they're fine rules." He was going to go insane if Shane didn't suck him already, but he knew instinctively that saying so would get him a longer wait.

"You learn quick," Shane told him, tearing open the condom. "It's all about control for me. Later, I'll beat off thinking about the way you had to strain to keep from reaching for me, how you came because I held you still and sucked you until you screamed."

John didn't know about the whole screaming when he came thing, but he was about to scream if Shane didn't get back to it.

Shane moved back a little. "Push your pants and boxers down so I can get to your balls, too."

John clumsily shoved the clothing down and put his hands back where he knew Shane wanted them.

"Good, so good for me."

That was kind of creepy, but John supposed it was part of Shane's kink. Shane murmured approvingly and took John's cock in hand at the base.

"You have a very nice dick, John."

"Thanks." John clenched his butt, trying not to beg. Shane touched the tip of his cock and smeared the pre-cum leaking from his slit around the glans. "Oh, oh, that's…"

Shane rolled the condom on, his hand gentle, pale against the darker flesh of John's cock.

As soon as Shane had him covered, he cupped John's balls and sucked John's crown into his mouth.

John moaned and watched as Shane took him in deep. He pressed John against the door with a forearm above

John's hip, then he hollowed his cheeks and proceeded to blow John's mind along with his dick.

Shane deep-throated him and even through the condom, John could feel those slick, warm muscles contracting around his shaft. He scratched at the door, shuffling his feet as he battled against thrusting.

Shane came back up and rolled his balls at the same time that he slapped his tongue over John's slit.

John's head hit the door as he jerked back, cursing softly. "Close," he got out, old habits from before he required condoms for getting head.

Shane tugged on his balls lightly and John registered a hint of pain—wasn't sure what he thought about it—then Shane took his cock in to the hilt, and John was coming, a low moan torn from him as his orgasm took him out of his head.

When he came back, Shane was taking the condom off and sporting a boner that John apparently wouldn't get to see.

"Can I get you a drink?" Shane asked. "Something cold before you go?"

John blinked then reached for his pants and boxers. "Nah." He cleared his throat. "No, it's…it's good. This was good." Weird, but he'd come pretty hard. It just seemed distant and cold after—"I, uh. We're good, right?"

Shane gave him a crooked smile. "Yeah. Don't hesitate to say hi, okay?"

John wasn't dense, not even after having half his brains sucked out. He knew a dismissal when heard it. Shane wasn't even interested in being friends. John couldn't claim to feel used, but he sure wondered what was wrong with him that he was drawing in guys who just wanted sex.

Stop being a hypocrite, he told himself. What the hell had he been doing before? Fucking anyone and everyone as long as they had the right parts. Really, was he doing anything different now?

John made sure his pants were up, zipped and buttoned, and his belt was in place, then he murmured goodbye and left. He needed to go home and seriously think about what he'd been doing this week, why he'd been doing it, and what he wanted. It was one thing to tell himself he wanted his forever man, and another thing entirely to act like he meant it.

He was pretty sure getting sucked off by one guy and getting a hand job by another in the same week put a lie to his claims. So what did he want?

John had left his briefcase in the truck. He wasn't comfortable leaving work documents out overnight, so he turned back and went out through the lobby. It surprised him to see that it was still light out. The sun set late this time of year, and he hadn't really been with Shane for all that long. It was odd how much could happen in such a short time.

He got his briefcase out of the truck and heard the buzz of an engine. John glanced to see what kind of car made such a tinny sound and found himself looking at Benji and the same guy who'd kissed him that morning, in the little car with the Corpus Christi plates.

If Benji looked his way, John couldn't tell. He averted his gaze and tried not to look that way again.

Whatever was going on between Benji and that guy, it had been more tender and had lasted longer than John's experience with Shane or Benji combined. How was it that he was the one looking for something more substantial— John stopped himself right there. The truth was, he hadn't been looking. He'd just…done like he used to, really, and had gone along with what the first two available guys had wanted.

Just because he wasn't drunk or stoned and wouldn't play without condoms now didn't mean he'd changed the things about him he'd thought he had. He'd bungled any chance he'd had with Benji, even to just be friends. The blow job from Shane had been great while it had been happening, but now he felt more alone than he had in a long while.

John locked up his truck and turned to walk back inside. He saw Benji and his friend going in ahead of him, so he slowed down, wanting them gone before he got inside.

They were, and the stairs were empty, too. John didn't have the energy to trot up them. His mood was darkening and he wavered over whether it was a situational thing or if he might be teetering toward a depressive episode. He'd have to watch himself closely, because even if he'd slipped slightly this week with the whole sex thing, he wasn't willing to let himself drown in a bout of depression. If he did, he might not make it out alive this time.

And he wouldn't think about Benji, who hadn't wanted anything but to get off with him, yet seemed to have someone who cared about him a great deal.

No, John wasn't going to think about that at all. He'd find a way to keep busy, maybe go drag Henry somewhere or hang out with Stacey and the kids. John took his keys out of his pocket and unlocked the door.

He stepped inside and felt like he'd been punched in the stomach when he saw the cream-colored paper on the floor.

Chapter Seven

John stared at the note for several minutes, his mind racing with conflicting thoughts. He hoped it was an attempt from Benji to perhaps be friends—and he hoped it was Benji telling him to fuck off and get on with his life.

It took an inordinate amount of willpower to make himself move. John shut and locked the door, then set down his briefcase. He bent and picked up the paper. It felt soft and carried the same scent as the first one. Did Benji spray the damn things with his cologne, like John had seen women do in old movies when they wrote love letters?

Is this a love letter? His fingers shook slightly and he stood. The urge to hold the note to his nose and sniff had him instead tucking it away in his shirt pocket. He was the one who was in control, not his emotions.

John picked up his briefcase again and went into his bedroom. It was stupid to think Benji had written anything other than a fuck-off note when John had just seen him with *that* guy, the kisser.

He put his briefcase beside the bed then kicked off his shoes. He felt grungy, and wasn't sure if it was an internal or external sensation, but thought a shower was in order either way.

The note—John couldn't keep pretending he wasn't dying to read it. He took it from his pocket and carefully unfolded it, as if something harmful might jump out at him from beneath the layers. Stupid, he knew, but then it occurred to him that for some reason, Benji did have the power to hurt him. How and when had that happened? More importantly, why?

John couldn't understand his reactions. He'd never gotten hung up on anyone quickly. There'd been two boyfriends, one that had lasted more than a year, but even so, it wasn't as if he'd fallen head over heels for either of them. Hell, John wasn't even sure he'd loved them. He'd been awfully young—eighteen and twenty—when each of those relationships had begun. Who knew anything about love at those ages, really?

Mom and Dad were married at eighteen. They know plenty about love. That was different. They were straight and—

"What the fuck," John muttered, stunned at his toxic train of thought. Did he really believe that, really believe only straight people fell in love like his parents did?

That can't be right. I... John thought about Henry, always picking losers then cheating on the only decent guy he'd ever dated. He thought about the men he'd been with, the ones he could remember.

Obviously there'd been a time when all he'd wanted was to get laid and to get out of his head. Had he subconsciously believed he'd never have the same intense love his parents had? Or his siblings had with their spouses?

Possibly. John racked his brain trying to think of any long-term gay couples he knew personally. The problem was, he'd only hung out with players like himself before, and with Henry, who was definitely not a good example. Again, had he deliberately put himself in with a crowd that would live up to his low expectations? John suspected that he had. Deep, life-long love was possible for anyone committed to it, regardless of gender. Thinking otherwise was just wrong, but he'd done a lot of things wrong.

Part of it was the depression fucking with him, making him feel as if he was worthless and unlovable, feelings he then reinforced by acting in a manner that kept him from being loved. John knew this, he did, after years of therapy. He just hadn't realized how far he'd gone to undermine his own happiness.

Blaming it all on his mental illness wasn't acceptable. John had to have some sort of control over it, or else he was nothing more than a puppet. Sometimes he slipped, sometimes his mood crashed, but he'd kept his head above the murky waters for some time now with only the occasional dunking to scare him.

Therapy or not, however, he hadn't been digging very deep to expose the ugly roots to his issues. John sighed and wished he had a beer. Surely just one wouldn't hurt, but since he had exactly zero types of alcohol in his place, wishing was a waste of time.

He needed to stop stalling. John finished unfolding the paper and took a deep breath before reading the words scrawled on the cream surface.

John,

Again, I'm resorting to the mature method of slipping a note under your door. I don't have your phone number – I can hardly apologize or try to explain anything if you run away. I know, I know. I ran, too, and it didn't help. It was a dumb thing to do. I am *sorry, for everything – pushing myself on you, throwing a fit.*

FYI, I wasn't making out with Derek in the lobby, it was just a hello kiss. How can you point fingers anyway when you were eye-fucking that older guy yesterday at the mailboxes? It doesn't matter. We need to at least be civil to each other, because Mrs. Royal and my grandpa are going to keep dating, and you and I will run into each other now and then.

Sincerely,
Benji Marks

"That's not passive-aggressive at all," John muttered, glaring at the paper like it'd personally offended him. Benji was just so…so confusing!

John was angry, and something very close to disappointed. He wanted to know who the hell Derek was and why he'd been kissing Benji like that, but he didn't have the right to ask. He also didn't understand why he even wanted to know in the first place.

Fed up with his own mental yammering and snarky thoughts, John set the note on the dresser and ran his hands through his hair, tugging on the short strands at the back until it hurt.

God, he was a mess, that was all there was to it. John rubbed his temples then. A cold shower would help. When he got done with that, he'd give Henry a call and see if he wanted to go see a movie or something. With his luck, Henry would be busy chasing some new guy down who'd fuck him then hurt him.

John showered, and his usual method for relaxing wasn't an option since he wasn't even horny. Despite the whole weird factor with Shane, the blow job had felt really good.

There was nothing wrong with that, either, John told himself. It was okay to have a little fun. He just needed to relax and stop being such an uptight jerk. Getting out and meeting people wouldn't hurt, either. John thought again about the church his mom had mentioned. Nagged him about, really. If he asked, Henry might go with him to check it out. Who knew, it might do them both some good at that point in their lives.

After he'd washed away the day's grunge, John shut off the shower and got out. A quick few swipes with the towel took care of most of the water dripping off him. He brushed his teeth and eyed his stubble. He'd have to shave before going back to work Monday, but he kind of liked the way he looked with the beginnings of a beard.

His hair was easy to tame with the comb, and it didn't take him more than ten minutes to finish getting ready. If Henry wasn't up to going out, John would take in a movie on his own or something. The idea of going to the theater alone kind of made him feel like a loser, but he could deal with it. Besides, there was a new action movie out with three Hollywood studs in it that seemed promising for lots of eye candy, no thinking required.

John glanced at the note and refused to acknowledge the twinge in his chest. He was making a big deal out of nothing.

Henry was at home moping when John called, and they arranged to meet at the Quarry movie theater. It was a compromise, as the outdoor shopping mall was almost smack dab between Henry's place and his. John actually preferred the theater where he could get a meal while he watched his movie, but Henry didn't care for it as he had an ex that worked there.

John locked up the apartment and left. He didn't see Benji anywhere, but John hardly looked for him, determined to get past the whole experience with Benji. Outside, the temperature was still close to unbearable. John strode to his truck, and before he realized what he was doing, he craned his neck, checking to see if Benji's car was still parked in the same spot.

It was, and he was a dumbass for looking. John turned his head back around before he walked into a vehicle or got hit. He unlocked his truck and got in, starting it immediately so the cold AC hit him full blast.

Traffic was about what he expected on a Friday night. The Quarry theater parking was packed, but he found a spot not completely out in the boonies and pulled into it. He shut the truck off, unbuckled then got out. The smell of exhaust fumes made him cringe as he had a vision of his lungs turning gray and shriveling up. He gave himself a mental eye roll and shut the truck door.

A honk startled him and he turned to see Henry with his window down, laughing at him. John flipped his friend off and yelled, "Good luck finding a spot to park your POS."

"This is a classic." Henry slapped the dash of the old Corolla — not a classic — then flipped him off right back. "Fits into compact spaces, too, not like that ugly truck of yours."

They both knew Henry lusted after the Tundra, not that he'd ever admit it. John flapped a hand at him. "I'll meet you up front." He turned and made his way to the theater, and saw that the line wound around the corner of the building. "Shit."

It should have occurred to him that there'd be the line from hell, considering the crowded parking lot. He checked the listings and saw that the movie they'd been intending to see was sold out through the midnight viewing.

"Damn it." Everything else was either a kid's flick or something he'd rather be tortured than watch.

"Great." Henry sighed behind him. "Guess we aren't the only ones who wanted to ogle some studs."

"Ya think?" John grumbled. "Well, now what?"

Henry poked his back. "We could try a different theater, or see one of the kid's movies."

John pivoted and shook his head. "No way in hell. We could go eat, I guess."

Henry rolled his eyes and huffed, "Fun. You've forgotten what it means."

"We had fun last weekend," John argued. "And I don't know that I'd call seeing a movie fun, exactly. It's a break from reality, but fun—"

"Jesus, stop taking everything so seriously. A movie can be fun, especially if you're seeing it with me." Henry eyed him speculatively. John didn't think he was going to like whatever Henry suggested instead of dinner out. Henry's predatory smile confirmed it. "We could go to this new club that opened a couple of months ago on the River Walk."

John was already shaking his head. "I don't do clubs anymore, Henry. You know that."

"Because you're scared of backsliding and having some good old-fashioned sex," Henry griped. "Your pecker is going to fall off from neglect."

John smirked at Henry. "It won't, since I've gotten off with two different guys this week. How often have you had another man jerking you off or sucking your dick this week, Henry?" As soon as he said it, John wanted to take the words back, but it was too late. Henry was staring slack-jawed and grabbing his elbow. John was propelled around the corner and into an area away from the people in line.

"Who?" Henry demanded. "I know you're not lying, because you look like you wished you'd kept your mouth shut—and"—Henry smacked John's arm— "how dare you hold out on me! Why didn't you call me and tell me about all this man sex you were having?"

John batted at Henry's hand when he would have whacked him again. "Cut it out, you horn dog." He sighed and leaned back against the wall. "I didn't tell you because I've been too busy freaking out, okay? I mean, come on, you know I haven't been messing around in years, then I start thinking maybe I should. Next thing I know, I've got a gorgeous, flaky guy in my lap, stroking me off, and two days after that, some older wannabe Dom-type sucking my dick but not letting me so much as touch him. It was a freaking weird week, and I just needed to decompress."

"You can decompress by telling me all the dirty details," Henry told him. "Come on, we're going to check out the jazz club and break you into clubs gently. You gotta learn to find your middle ground, John. It doesn't have to be all or nothing. You're not either a sinner or a saint, a slut or abstinent—though I'll give you obstinate, that you are, bud."

"Jerk." John felt the truth of the words, though.

"Whatever. Just like you're scared shitless to step into a gay club again, afraid you'll turn into some sex-crazed slut. Phtp." Henry waved the idea off. "How are you ever gonna know you're different now if you don't try?"

"Why put myself in the path of temptation?" John asked.

Henry frowned at him. "What are you doing? Was that from the Bible or something?"

"Maybe, but that's not what I was thinking of. I was thinking, if I know I have a weakness, why risk it?"

"You don't know that you have a weakness. Shit, John, it was a combination of things that made you the way you used to be, and now you're doing better, kind of, but you're never going to trust yourself any if you don't know that you've changed." Henry held up one finger when John opened his mouth to argue. "No, don't even. You used sex and booze and God knows what else to escape from life before, now you just do it by refusing to leave your apartment unless it's the weekly family dinner—sorry for bailing on that, but I had to work late—or hanging out with me, the 'safe' gay guy."

John was stuck by the truth Henry had seen and he hadn't. How was it that his friend could be so blind about his own life and yet see John's issues so clearly? *Then again, I can point out Henry's problems easy enough, can't I?*

"Even messing around with guys this week, I bet that was at your place, wasn't it?" Henry asked.

"Uh." John frowned. "Well, with Benji, yeah, but Shane was at his place."

"Same apartments?" Henry arched an eyebrow at him.

"Yeah, but we did go to Starbucks first." That had to count for something.

"Doesn't count," Henry informed him. "Nope, because I bet you didn't call it a date, not at first, and Starbucks is right the fuck there by where you live."

John scowled at his friend. "Now dates have to take place a certain distance from one's residence to be classified as an actual date?"

"Was it a date? Or were you meeting for coffee, just kind of feeling each other out?"

"That's still a date," John argued. "Yes, it is," he reiterated when Henry disagreed. "It is, too. We agreed it was a date while we were both sitting there, and we weren't there long because Shane and I decided to go to his place, where I got the weirdest, maybe the best, blow job I've ever had."

"The control thing you mentioned." Henry nodded. "Did he tie you up or anything?"

"No!" John barked. "I would never let some guy I didn't know very well do that to me now." Before he'd been an anything goes type of guy, but not now.

"Okay, okay, calm the fuck down. What about this Benji guy?"

John bit his lip and hated that he felt so many confusing things just on hearing Benji's name. He couldn't even sort them out, but maybe talking about it would help. "Can we go somewhere and talk? Besides a bar, or club, whatever."

Henry gave the most put-upon sounding sigh John had ever heard from him. "Fine, let's go back to your place. We can order pizza."

"I don't want to have to shout," John explained, but Henry gave him a knowing look.

"Sure, because it's not like you couldn't sit beside me and talk, and you know how jazz clubs are. They have those zany trumpeters blowing their horn right in your ear."

John actually had no idea what a jazz club was like, but he was quite familiar with Henry's sarcasm. "Asshole."

"Two peas in a pod and all those other trite sayings that mean you, too."

They walked back to John's truck, and John ended up giving Henry a ride over to his car. "See you in a few."

Henry waved at him and John navigated around an idiot driving the wrong way down the lane. "Can't you tell by the way the cars are parked that you're going the wrong way?" he muttered, cringing when he thought his truck was about to get dinged. When the other car scooted past, he loosened his grip on the steering wheel and cursed as blood flowed back into his fingers.

Henry seemed to want to play street racer on the highway, but John refused to accelerate every time Henry pulled up beside him and honked. Once he made sure there wasn't a problem, that it was just Henry being immature like he could be, John turned up his radio and ignored his friend until they were both parked and out of their vehicles.

A laugh that sent tingling sensations to his balls had John looking across the lot. He grabbed Henry's arm when Henry would have started walking toward the building.

"What—" Henry started but John hissed at him to hush. There weren't as many cars parked outside as it was a weekend night and people were out doing weekend things. John spotted Benji easily, and glowered when he saw a different guy chattering away to Benji.

"Which one is him, and which him is he?"

"Huh?" John would have glared at Henry, but he couldn't quite look away from Benji. He was beside one of the lamp posts so that the light from it shone down on him like he was some divine creature. His dark hair glinted, and his clothes were just tight enough to show off his very fine form.

"Ah, so that one is Benji," Henry whispered. "You're drooling."

"Am not," John snapped, wiping at his mouth automatically.

"Gotcha. Come on, let's go inside and you can tell me about the little stud."

John smirked at Henry. "He's not exactly little all over."

Henry gave him a narrow look. "Don't tease me like that or I'll beat off in your bathroom. You'd better have some juicy details when we get inside."

John was afraid Henry would end up slapping one out in the bathroom anyway, but it probably wouldn't have been the first time. Inside the lobby, John saw Shane talking to another man, and he wondered if Shane was working the guy like he'd worked John.

That's not fair. I agreed to everything. When had he become such a judgmental prick?

"This place has got the ugliest carpet," Henry muttered.

John glanced down, though he knew Henry was right. "Well, you hear about the vet whose pet doesn't get taken care of, or the child psychiatrist whose kids are proof that Satan is alive and well and breeds with humans. It's kind of like that. I don't give a shit about carpet unless I'm trying to sell it." In fact, he kind of found the orange and gray patterned carpeting he was walking on comforting. It meant he was almost home.

"It's fucking hideous, dude. It's…offensive. I could probably sue the owners of the place for causing pain and suffering to my eyeballs."

"Here I thought I was being the drama mama, but you've got that title owned." John led them to the stairwell door, where Henry whined.

"Aw, come on. I'm tired and hungry. I'm gonna take the elevator."

John grabbed his elbow. "No, I don't think so. I distinctly remember promising you when I moved in here to make sure you took the steps with me so you'd keep your ass in fine shape."

Henry peered over his shoulder, trying to eye his own ass. "It looks fine from this angle."

John swatted him and Henry yelped. "Get moving, Henry, before I spank you again."

Henry batted his lashes and folding his hands together against his chest. "Oh, would you please, you bad boy?"

"Dork," John got out before laughing. Henry was such a goof, but already John felt better than he had in days. "Come on, see if you can keep up." He thought he heard other voices, but Henry let out a whoop and got in a payback swat as John took off.

"I can see the stairs have helped you out. Buns of steel, man."

John didn't reply, jogging as fast as he dared because he knew Henry was going to be trying to pass him any second.

Sure enough, Henry bumped him and John nearly tripped. "Hey!"

Henry cackled.

John stopped at the second floor landing and let Henry go first. "There's something to be said with finishing last," he called out with a bit of smugness. Yeah, he was feeling better than he'd thought he would. Maybe he was making some progress after all.

Chapter Eight

His head felt like someone had stuffed it full of rocks. Hot, pounding rocks. John groaned and tried not to move as it throbbed violently. God, what had he done?

Then he became aware of a loud, sawing sound, and it came back to him. He and Henry had talked and laughed halfway through the night. Henry had gone to the corner convenience store and bought a twelve-pack of Bud before the pizza had arrived, and John had proceeded to get shit-faced.

He most certainly hadn't whined about Benji to Henry. That was one of those false-memories he'd heard about. John forced himself to open one eye, and when that didn't kill him, he slowly opened the other. The bedroom was dark, but not pitch black as the blinds and curtains only kept out so much of the morning sun. What slipped in around the edges here and there was enough to help John navigate his way to the bathroom once he got up.

Henry was still snoring when John came out of the bathroom, freshly showered and feeling somewhat human. He tiptoed out of the bedroom with the bath towel around his hips still, unwilling to risk waking Henry up should he make too much noise.

Of course, with the way Henry was snoring, John figured he probably could have sung the national anthem at the top of his lungs and not disturb him. In the kitchen, he made a pot of coffee and contemplated whether or not he wanted to eat breakfast. He didn't, but toast was probably a good idea.

They'd left the pizza out overnight, the lid open and while John didn't think he had any roaches in the place, he was leery of eating the pizza. With his luck, he'd get food poisoning and end up in the hospital.

"Toast it is." He took a couple of slices of bread and put them in the toaster. Then he saw the note lying on the table and his heart did a little flip right along with his stomach.

It was the same note from the day before. For a split second, he'd hoped... But that was stupid. He'd showed it to Henry, who'd promptly started teasing him about having a guy named after a dog panting at him. John hadn't known what the hell Henry was talking about until he'd explained Benji was the name of a dog in a movie.

John didn't remember a whole lot after that. At least there hadn't been any puking. That was the worst.

His toast popped up and John set about buttering it while the coffee pot finished percolating. He had a cup of coffee per slice of toast, and his head wasn't nearly as stuffy as it had been. John poured himself a third cup then wandered into the living room and turned on the

TV. There likely wouldn't be anything on, but that was okay. He just needed to veg out.

Once he'd settled in on the couch, John let himself look toward the door. There was no note. No surprise, he guessed. What more was there to be said? Or written? "Or snarled." He'd done that when he'd last spoken at Benji.

John flipped channels and finally ended up leaving the TV on A & E. Maybe he'd get to watch reruns of the show with the duck people on it. His mind wandered, and he tried to figure out some of the questions he'd been asking himself lately. Did he believe he could actually have his happily ever after?

The answer to that one shocked him. He wondered if he *deserved* a happy ever after. Why was he so hard on himself? What was up with that level of self-loathing? If anyone had asked him if he hated himself, he'd have said no without doubting it. But for him to think he didn't deserve to be happy was just fucked up.

Had he really been doing like Henry had said, hiding away and pretending he was all better, when in reality, he wasn't? John ran it around and around in his thoughts. He'd denied himself any real pleasure for the past couple of years—and any real sexual pleasures. Why?

For one, he didn't want to keep sticking his dick in every available orifice that came his way. It had been an ego rush, then it had been a necessity to keep that same ego fed. When he'd spiraled into a depressive state, he'd searched for that boost by fucking more, caring less, and in return, he'd only sunk deeper into depression. It had been a degrading repetitive cycle he hadn't known how to get out of.

If he hadn't had a moment of clarity after bare-backing some faceless stranger one night, he wouldn't have freaked out and accidentally dialed Robert's number. He'd been trying for Henry, but with all the alcohol he'd consumed, everything had been blurry.

He'd been able to hear, though, and when the guy he'd fucked had got dressed to leave like John had asked him to — or told him to, that part was blurry, too — John had heard well enough the suggestion he get tested for AIDS.

It had scared the shit out of him. Like everyone his age in developed countries, John knew the risks of unprotected sex. It just hadn't seemed like a real risk once he'd been in the cycle where he wanted to give in and let the darkness take him. He wouldn't have actively killed himself.

Yes, John had to accept that he *would* have, because that unprotected sex had been like playing Russian roulette. Maybe, if a couple had been together a while and were truly committed to each other, then that was different. They could get tested, make the promise never to cheat, never to risk the other's life. But fucking indiscriminately like he'd done, using condoms only when the other guy wanted him to… No one had to tell John how lucky he was. He knew. He *knew*.

How many men had he had unprotected sex with? That, he didn't have an answer to, not necessarily because there'd been so many, simply because he couldn't remember specifics when he'd been so drunk or high. It had taken him two years of testing to believe he wasn't going to pop up with HIV. He didn't know if he'd ever be willing to have unprotected sex again, that was the truth. It wasn't a bad thing, either, as far as he was concerned.

Another thing was, he wanted to like himself. Henry had been right about a lot of things. Dr. Hannah had been helpful, but at some point, John had started telling her what he thought he should be saying, not necessarily what he felt. All his smug idealism, his pride, had been misplaced. He'd been hiding for the past two years, not healing.

John closed his eyes and leaned his head back, trying to formulate a plan. Going out to clubs might prove he had self-control now, but he doubted he'd meet the kind of man he wanted to there. Still, if he could go just to dance and have fun, that might be okay. He just had to be careful not to let being wanted make him a slut again.

That was part of the root of it. It made him feel good to be wanted, but he suspected being loved and with someone who respected him would make him feel a hell of a lot better than good.

Benji had wanted him to get off with, and so had Shane... Well, Shane had wanted to control his orgasm and get John off, then be a selfish prick and jerk off alone, denying John the reassurance that he'd pleased the jerk. *Or something like that.*

It was confusing trying to sort it all out, especially with a hangover still making him feel sluggish. All he really could conclude was that he needed to start trying to have a more fulfilling life — and that he probably owed Benji an apology. John had crossed a line yesterday, snapping at Benji for being with that guy. *Derek.* John snorted. Okay, he'd been a complete asshole, and when had Benji seen him talking with Shane before that?

He groaned again and raised his head up, opening his eyes. His coffee was probably cold. John picked up the cup and took a sip. "Nasty." Henry was still snoring loud enough to be heard in the living room. John hadn't paid attention before, but he had to wonder if Henry had sleep apnea or maybe a small rodent sleeping in his nose and blocking the proper airflow. With all of the racket he was making, it wouldn't have been surprising.

His stomach wasn't trying to crawl up his throat, so John got up and went back to the kitchen for more coffee. He topped off the cold with hot, then put the whole cup in the microwave. While he watched the seconds tick off, he tried to think of what to say to Benji. 'I'm sorry I was a total ass' seemed the best.

The idea of talking to Benji was intimidating, and yet John couldn't deny that it was also stimulating. Not only in a sexual way—because thinking about Benji gave him a hard-on in no time at all—but because he didn't know what would happen, and *that* was exciting.

The microwave dinged and John pushed the button to open the door. When he took out his coffee, he noticed some sort of foodstuff stuck to the glass. He squinted at the splotch, but for the life of him couldn't tell what it was. If he didn't clean it up, it might turn into some kind of radioactive waste.

His imagination was working just fine. John sipped his coffee and walked to the sink to get the dish sponge. After he wiped up the spot of what he thought might be cheese, John tossed the sponge back in the vicinity of the sink. He drank the rest of his coffee then set the cup on the counter.

Rash decisions weren't wise, he told himself. It didn't matter. He was going to see if Benji could talk for a few minutes. John knew where Mr. Marks' apartment was.

He shouldn't have worried about his appearance since he was only going to apologize, but John went to the bathroom and checked his hair. Brushing his teeth wasn't a bad idea in case he had toast stuck in between them somewhere so he did that, too. It was for hygiene purposes, not because there was going to be any kissing.

There wouldn't, John told himself firmly. Benji already had someone else to mess around with. Possibly two more guys, considering the one in the parking lot from last night. Whoever the new guy was, he'd been even shorter than Benji, and dark-headed.

Don't think about it. All I'm going to do is apologize and try to reach a truce. Benji sort of extended the olive branch with the second note. Being cordial was all well and good, but cordial sounded like such an old word, as if only old people did it. John could see Mr. Marks being cordial to someone, but when he tried applying the word to him or Benji, he suddenly pictured them as old and stooped.

John just liked the idea of being friendly better. Friendly implied smiles and laughing, and Benji had a great laugh. Cordial—there was a distance implied in the word to him.

Questioning why distance would be a problem could wait for later. John left the bathroom after one last glance. He looked like a guy, nothing special, but that was okay. He dressed quickly—a simple T-shirt, jeans and flip flops—taking extra care not to make a lot of noise. Henry snored on, and John jotted a quick note for him on one of the pizza place's napkins. Henry should see it on the table if he got up before John returned.

John tucked his keys and cell phone in his jeans pocket and left the apartment. He almost ran right over some guy he didn't know. "Sorry. I didn't mean to bump into you."

The man grumbled but kept walking. John watched him for a second then shrugged. The guy didn't look familiar but he didn't know everyone who lived on his floor.

Mr. Marks' apartment was on the first floor, like Mrs. Royal's. Why hadn't he even thought of that when he'd slipped into Shane's place? Benji might have seen him and thought—

Doesn't matter what he thought if he saw us. He has his...friends.

Was that the kind of friend John wanted to be with Benji? As much as he wanted to say no, his dick was saying yes, growing erect just from thinking about it. Damn it, he was drawn to Benji, and Benji was an unknown, really. John didn't know him at all. Maybe they could change that.

John knocked on the door and waited. After two minutes had passed, he debated knocking again, but if anyone was in there asleep, he didn't want to wake them. He put his hand to the heavy door and rested his brow against it, too. He'd really wanted to talk to Benji, and the let-down was greater than it should have been.

John forced himself to turn around and walk away. He kept his eyes trained on the ugly carpet but he didn't really see anything. The sounds of doors opening and closing, people chatting, barely registered.

"John!"

John froze mid-step, then thought of how ridiculous he must look and he put his foot down before turning around. Because he knew that voice, and he was very glad he'd put on a long T-shirt that covered his resurging hard-on.

He watched as Benji stood in the doorway to Mr. Marks' place, chewing on his bottom lip. Benji wouldn't look right at him, and John had almost given up on them talking when Benji stepped out into the hall and closed the door. He glanced almost shyly at John. "Did you... Did you need something?"

John stopped walking—he hadn't even realized he was moving toward Benji until then. He cleared his throat and hoped his voice didn't crack. "Yeah, I, uh—" The tenant beside Mr. Marks came out of her place and looked at them for a moment before going back inside. "Maybe we could go somewhere and talk for a few minutes?"

Benji glanced at the door behind him as if considering going back inside. John's pulse raced and he prepared himself for the embarrassment of being told no.

"Your place?" Benji asked instead, still not meeting his gaze.

John refrained from letting out a whoop. "Ah, my—" Bringing up Henry's name might not be the best idea. John didn't want Benji to get the wrong idea.

Benji looked at him then and John was afraid he had a guilty expression, though he'd done nothing wrong. "Coffee? If you...if you'd like, we could go to Starbucks."

"Won't it be hard to have a conversation there?" Benji asked.

It probably would. "We could go out back to the courtyard." John almost never thought of the little grassy area because if he wanted to go outside, he wanted to be hiking or fishing, not sitting on a bench, staring at flowers.

Benji's forehead puckered with a wrinkle as his expression shifted into one of confusion. "We have a courtyard here?"

"That's what they call it, but it's just a dinky spot."

Benji finally came toward him, looking so serious. "Okay then. Let's get this over with."

That didn't sound good at all. John was silent as he showed Benji the way to the courtyard. Outside, the morning air was already heavy with humidity and the sun was warming everything up entirely too much. John found the one bench in the shade of a pecan tree and gestured Benji to sit.

"I'll stand, thanks," Benji said quietly.

John blew out a nervous breath and sat down. Benji stayed a few feet away, shifting his weight from foot to foot, and John suddenly understood that Benji was nervous, too. For some reason, knowing he wasn't the only one made him feel better, and it was easier to speak.

"I wanted to tell you I'm sorry for yesterday," John said. Benji did look at him then, those big dark eyes filled with something John couldn't decipher. "I just wasn't—I haven't been around men in"—he dropped his voice to a whisper—"a sexual way, haven't been interested for a while." He tried a little half smile to see if Benji would relax. The man looked so tightly wound, John halfway expected him to snap. Benji blinked, but that was it, so John forged on.

"I used to be pretty wild, and very reckless. I have..." John swallowed, forced himself to go on, "I have some problems I don't really want to get into." Not when he wasn't even sure they'd be friends after this. "I've been thinking about things, and I—the other day, when you got on my lap"—God, John's dick was achingly hard—

"it had been over two years since someone else had touched me. I was kind of stunned and stupid after coming." He could have added confused and misguided, but that was more than needed to be said, because Benji was beginning to edge closer. It was like getting a spooked animal to trust him. Not a nice analogy, and not a hundred percent accurate, but it was the best John could come up with.

"You said you weren't looking for anything serious, and see, I didn't want to end up being the way I used to be before."

Benji held up a hand. "But you hooked up with that guy, didn't you? The old one."

John wished he could tell what Benji was thinking before he answered, but lying wasn't the right thing to do. "Well, kind of, I guess. We didn't, we didn't fuck, it wasn't that kind of hook up."

"But you want something more long-term than just screwing around?" Benji asked, shaking his head. "Help me out here, John, because that seems like a contradiction."

"You were with someone else," John couldn't help but point out. "I'm not judging, just stating what I saw." Not judging on the outside maybe, not verbally, but inside it made him angry and that wasn't right. John shoved the ugly feeling down. "You and Derek, kissing, then last night you were in the parking lot with someone else."

Boy, when Benji did that wrinkling up of his nose thing, he was just adorable. Benji seemed completely unaware of it as he spoke. "Derek is an ex. He's the reason I don't want serious right now. Three years with him cheating on me while I was such a fucking idiot believing the excuses he gave me."

"But—" John had seen the way Derek touched Benji, the way he kissed him. "He—it—the way he kissed you—" He couldn't articulate what he was trying to say, but Benji sighed and sat down beside him.

"John, you ought to know that not everything you see is true." Benji brushed a speck of lint off his black pants. "Actions speak louder than words and all that shit, but not always. Actions can lie, too. I don't doubt that Derek wishes he had me back. He's asked me often enough to make me crazy the past couple of days, but he's got to understand that he lost me. No." Benji shook his head. "He threw me away, threw us away, just so he could stick his dick in as many other guys' asses as possible. Unlike your old guy, Derek is all about anal."

That was more than John needed to know, but he kept quiet as Benji sat beside him, talking.

"I left Corpus to get away from him. He's not evil, not a stalker, either. I probably wasn't as clear as I could have been that he'd never get me back." He hitched one shoulder in a shrug. "I was a bit pissed off when I found out about him cheating. I spent three years being faithful, and all the time he was screwing around. You know how I found out?"

"No." John wasn't sure he wanted to know, but damned if he'd speak up.

Benji grimaced and his cheeks turned ruddy. "I snooped. It's wrong and all that shit, unless your life is at risk. I had this kid, couldn't have been much over eighteen, anyway, he came up to me and informed me that Derek had said he was a better lay and I should expect to get dumped any day. I was fucking dumbfounded, and at work at the museum. I couldn't just go off on the kid, and my shift had just started. I had all day to stew over what that little fuck told me.

"At first I tried to rationalize it. The kid was jealous, lying, whatever. But there was something in his smug expression, made me want to kill him and believe him, or the other way around. Once I could think, I just knew."

Benji inhaled, let it out shakily. "So I went home and Derek, he works at the science museum, he was staying late for some project," Benji snorted. "Right. A young, barely legal project who was damned lucky I didn't brain him. Anyway, I snooped. Got on the desktop we shared, accessed his emails and messages. I don't think Derek ever thought I'd look, or else he wanted me to, I don't know. His passwords were all the same, his name and birth date—and he'd told me that, back when we'd first moved in together.

"Everything was right there," Benji rasped, blinking rapidly. "Right the fuck there on the desktop. He had pictures, lots and lots of them. I knew they were from after we got together because he got this anchor tattoo right after we decided to live together. That tattoo on his hip showed in a lot of the pictures. I thought I loved him, but I guess I didn't love him enough. I couldn't stay."

John wanted to smack the crap out of Derek, but the part about fucking everything, it sounded so much like himself, like he used to be, and he'd confessed that to Benji minutes earlier. What must Benji think of him?

"So, I waited until he came home, and I could smell it—sex." Benji turned a knowing look on him. "Even if there's condoms used, you can still smell it, you know?"

"Yeah," John agreed, thinking of yesterday.

"I just, I just lost it, and Derek tried to deny everything." Benji sighed and rolled his eyes. "He just would *not* admit it until I put the computer program on slideshow. Then it was all my fault for snooping."

"What an asshole," John couldn't help but say.

"Yeah, but the thing is, and here's what fucks with my head. Derek's not all bad. He was really sweet, and he could be the most compassionate person I've ever met. He just couldn't keep his dick in his pants, or my ass, whatever."

John winced, wishing he hadn't heard that last part. "When did this happen?"

"About a month ago. I kind of took a road trip, visited some friends in Mexico before coming to stay with Gramps. Mexico was really nice, but I couldn't live there. Yesterday was the first time I'd seen Derek since I'd left. I decided, rather than be angry and keep letting that poison me, I'd just let him go." Benji's laugh had a bitter twang to it. "He didn't want to be let go. Promised he'd be faithful and go to therapy, anything if I'd just come back. I didn't go, obviously. That's why I said I guess I didn't love him enough. I don't feel anything but sad that I wasted three years with someone who was such a ho. Someone I obviously didn't know like I thought I did."

Did Benji think he was the same way? Maybe not before their current talk, but John bet he did now. "People can change," he said softly, and he had to believe that, didn't he?

"Maybe. I still could never trust him again, you know? I said I don't feel anything besides being sad, but that's not all. I have a lot of anger, and honestly, I was probably trying to work some of that out on you."

John leaned away from Benji and tried not to be hurt that Benji had been using him, or trying to. He sure hadn't objected when Benji had been writhing on his lap.

"Most guys don't have a problem with getting laid, so I figured you'd be okay with it too." Benji looked up at the sky, and John did too, only to stop when he didn't see what Benji was seeing — something that must have been in his head. "You kind of didn't just fall into line with my plans to get out and have as much meaningless sex as possible." He laughed, looking at John, and something warm raced through him. John told himself it was just heat from the sun.

Benji laughed again and touched John's arm. "So I found the one guy who isn't interested in screwing around, and the thing is..." He moved over on the bench until his hip was against John's. Then he looked up at John through those thick black lashes and when Benji spoke, his voice was a bare rasp. "The thing is, I think I could like you, John. I still want you sexually, that's a given, but I think, if things were different and I wasn't trying to get over three years of being lied to and cheated on, that I could..."

John's heart fluttered as Benji tipped his chin up and parted his lips. John knew it was a bad idea, and a worse action, but he dipped his head and slanted his mouth over Benji's. Benji moaned and John's eyelids slid closed as he gently twined his tongue with Benji's.

It was like coming back to a place he knew was safe and good. John stopped trying to think about what they were doing and instead fitted his hands to Benji's waist. Benji twisted and got his chest partially pressed to John's, and he ran his hands up John's torso.

Everything about Benji felt right, tasted right, sounded right. John wanted him with an intensity he'd not felt before. Not that he could recall. He moved one hand around to Benji's back then went up further until he cupped Benji's nape.

He held Benji and kissed him deeper, a little roughly, needing something he couldn't describe. The sun couldn't match the heat building between them. John's senses were filled with Benji, immersing him in the confounding, hurt man in his arms.

Benji curled his fingers against John, scratching him through his shirt and making his chest sting in a way that had him wanting to bend Benji over the bench and fuck him senseless. It was only the sound of a child squealing happily that shoved John back to reality and out of the sensual bubble he had been in with Benji. He pulled back reluctantly and Benji tried to drag him close again.

"Kid," John warned, catching Benji's hands in his. They were in Texas, and making out in public wasn't ever a wise thing to do. John was just glad he'd heard the little squeaker who came running around the curved sidewalk past the shrubs to where they were sitting. He let go of Benji's hands just in time to keep from being busted.

"Hi!" the little girl said, running right up to them. John would put her at about four. She was adorable, with her black curly hair and pretty brown eyes.

"Velva, don't go running off, I've told you — Oh!" The girl's mama stopped and looked at them. "I'm sorry. I didn't know anyone would be out here." She looked at her daughter. "Velva, don't bother the men."

"She wasn't," John assured the mother. "She just said hi. She's cute." He winked at Velva and the little girl giggled, blinking both eyes as she tried to wink back.

"Hi," Benji said, and John noticed his voice lacked some of its usual verve. He glanced at Benji, who gave him a helpless look. He guessed Benji didn't know anything about kids.

"Hi!" Velva tried her blink-winks on Benji.

"She's winking at you," John whispered.

"Uh, okay."

He assumed Benji winked back because Velva giggled, bringing out dimples in her cheeks.

"She won't leave you alone once you talk to her," her mama warned, walking over to stand by her child.

Velva began running around the pecan tree, singing some song John thought she might have made up while John smiled at the girl's mom and held out his hand. "That's okay. I'm John Weston, and this is Benji Marks."

"Destiny Ochoa, and you've met Velva." They shook, then Destiny and Benji shook hands as well. "So do you have kids?"

"Nah," John said. "Just lots of nieces and nephews from my brothers and sisters."

She gave him a knowing look but didn't seem inclined to think he was the spawn of all that was evil in the universe. "What about you?"

Benji jerked like he'd been poked in the ribs. "I uh, no, no kids."

Destiny grinned and chuckled a little before sitting on the bench beside theirs. "You seem a little nervous there, Benji. Haven't been around many kids?"

"Not since I grew up," Benji quipped. Then he seemed to loosen up. "We had school tours through the museum I used to work at in Corpus though, so they aren't totally foreign creatures to me."

That got him another chuckle from Destiny, and soon the three of them were talking as if they'd known each other for longer than just a few minutes.

It was a good morning, John decided, watching Benji animatedly explain a display at the museum he'd worked at, waving his hands in the air while Destiny laughed and Velva wink-blinked at him. A much better morning than he'd had for a long time.

Chapter Nine

Velva decided she was hungry after a half an hour or so of playing. John and Benji watched her and Destiny leave, then John tried to calm the butterflies in his belly as he turned to look at Benji. Would they resume where they'd left off, maybe back at his place? John could explain who Henry was — but would Benji believe him, after his own confessions and Benji's experience with Derek?

Benji pursed his lips as if considering something. "The other guy last night, he wasn't just a friend though."

John's butterflies turned to lead and dropped heavily in his stomach. "He wasn't?" he got out.

"No." Benji still wasn't looking at him. "He was just someone to get off with. It was okay."

"I don't need a rundown of it," John snapped. He closed his eyes and tried to get control of himself. "Sorry."

"It's okay."

Benji sounded strange, but when John dared to peek at him he couldn't see that anything was off. "No. I mean, I told you about Shane—"

"Shane?" There was that puckering of Benji's lips again. "That's a horrible name. It's like an old guy name."

John let out a snort before he could stop himself. "That's ageism or something, I'm sure."

"Whatever." Benji shrugged. "I don't like him."

John wanted desperately to ask if it was because of him, but couldn't bring himself to do so. He knew how he felt about Derek and the guy in the parking lot. John wanted to punch them both.

Benji kicked at the ground. "But, you can see him again, I'm not saying anything like you can't. I mean, I'm attracted to you, duh, but there's still a lot of shit I'm dealing with. I'm not ready for anything heavy."

John wouldn't let the pain show. It shouldn't hurt, anyway. Benji wasn't outright rejecting him. But... "What does that mean, for us?"

Benji stopped toeing the ground but still didn't look at John when he answered. "Well, I'd like to take you back to my place, but it's Gramps' place not mine, and he's open-minded but I'm not sure he's that open-minded. How about your place?"

John started to agree, then remembered Henry, sleeping in his bed. He was afraid this was going to end badly. Still, he cupped Benji's chin and urged him to turn his head. Benji's resistance only lasted a moment, then he met John's gaze.

"The thing is, I'm afraid you won't believe me when I say this, but it's the truth." God, he hoped he was wrong and Benji didn't think he was a liar. "There's my best friend, Henry, asleep in my bed. We didn't—we don't ever do anything together, not anything sexual, I swear."

Benji had quit looking at him before he finished the second sentence, but he hadn't pulled away.

"Benji, I mean it. He's my friend, and he'll tell you that, too."

Waiting for Benji to speak or show him something, some feeling at all, was going to give John an ulcer. He'd swear his stomach was burning already. Benji moved and pulled his chin free. He stood, still not looking at John.

"Benji—" John began, but Benji grunted and *that* didn't sound good. John had no choice but to be patient, and finally Benji walked a few feet away. John thought for sure he was about to run off again, but Benji surprised him by turning back around and striding right up to him.

"Here's the thing, John," Benji said after gulping. "I have no right to be bothered by that, and there's no reason for me to care if you're lying or not. I mean, I can't handle a relationship right now. My head is too fucked up."

John would bet Benji's heart was battered too, but Benji wouldn't admit it. "It is the truth, though. I know with what I told you about the way I used to be, and then Shane and—" John realized he wasn't doing himself any favors. He shut up.

Benji cocked his head to the right and pursed his lips again, then he almost smiled. "I think maybe I believe you, but the fact is, it shouldn't matter to me either way, and it does. That bothers me more than anything else right now. We should just want to fuck. *I* should just want to fuck. According to your history, same thing. It's just confusing."

"For me, too," John admitted. "I thought about you all week. It pissed me off that I thought about you all week, too."

Benji fluttered his lashes and smiled seductively. "I do have that effect on people."

"Tease," John said, taking a swat at his hip.

Benji leaped aside and waved a finger at him. "Nuh-uh, no damaging the goods."

John laughed despite the need coiling in his groin. "Dork."

"I'm too good lookin' to be a dork," Benji told him.

"Not true, dorks are the studs right now."

"Whatever."

John wanted to touch Benji, to take his hand and just hold it, but Benji had to let him know such a thing would be okay.

Benji tucked his hands in his front pockets, which was an answer in itself. He kept his head down a little, yet looked up at John. "The thing is, John, I think you're right to want to step away from me. I'm…I'm hot and cold. I want you, but I don't want to be with just you. I'm sorry if that's hurtful but I can't promise to be good to anyone right now, but I will be honest."

It did hurt, so much that John couldn't even speak. Benji dug the toe of his shoe into the dirt.

"I don't think I can say no to you if you ask me, either. I don't want to say no."

John's gut tightened with lust at Benji's words.

"So if you want, we could have a physical relationship, be friends with benefits, maybe. I liked talking with you this morning."

Oh God. John's desire for Benji rushed through him. "So you just want the fucking?"

"We don't have to do that," Benji said quickly, "anything is good, if we do it together. I mean, I think anything we did together would be good, as long as we don't include animals and most types of food."

That startled a laugh out of John before he said, "No, no animals, and we can negotiate the food types." Which was when he knew he was going to go along with anything Benji wanted him for.

Benji beamed at him. "Okay, then. We'll do that. But John?"

"Yeah?"

"I—" Benji glanced away, then focused on him. "We are clear on the terms, right? You can fuck around, I can too. We aren't dating. We aren't anything but friends who get off with each other sometimes."

John didn't like it, but he liked the idea of no Benji at all even less. "Okay."

Benji stepped closer. "So you'll date other people?" he asked earnestly.

John didn't want to, but if it made Benji happy to think so, then he'd agree. "Yeah." Plus, he might end up meeting someone who was right for him, someone who could get him past Benji since Benji wasn't interested in more. John understood where Benji was coming from. He didn't blame him, either.

"Safe sex, even for blow jobs," John added to their list of agreements.

"I'm actually okay with that. Derek insisted, and now I know why. Sorry, I probably shouldn't mention him."

John disagreed. "Why not? You said we would be friends, too, so shouldn't you be able to talk to me?"

"I guess. Just seems weird." Benji moved a little closer. "So, do you think you could get your friend to take a hike, or at least move to the floor?"

"I can drag his hungover ass to the couch if it means you'll come back with me."

"It does," Benji said. "I can even help you drag him."

John took Benji by the elbow and gave him a brief, fierce kiss.

"Oh, my," Benji gasped, fanning himself.

John grinned and steered Benji inside then to the stairs.

"Want to watch me again?" Benji asked.

John figured his growl was answer enough. Benji took off, working that round ass of his like a pro.

By the time they reached the third floor, John was ready to take Benji there in the stairwell. The only reason he didn't try was because they had neither condoms nor lube.

As soon as they got to John's door, John took out his keys and unlocked the deadbolts. "Inside," he rasped, then he was following Benji in, grabbing the man by his shoulders and hauling him around for a kiss that made John's insides quiver.

John pinned Benji to the door and began plundering his mouth, thrusting into the warmth there while rutting against Benji's hip.

"Oh, oh fuck," Benji whimpered, grabbing at his arms, then his hips, then back to his arms. "Fuck me."

John had something else in mind. He didn't think he could fuck Benji and stay detached.

Like I'm detached now?

John told that inner voice to fuck off. He dragged Benji closer to him and kept kissing him, touching him with as much of his own body as possible.

"Guys, if y'all will let me out, I'll leave y'all to it."

Benji squeaked at the deep voice, and tried to shove himself through the door, but John turned his head enough to glare at Henry.

"Just trying to help, but I can watch—"

John held onto Benji, afraid he'd bolt. "Henry, I swear—"

"Often, yes, you do. Your mama's gonna soap your mouth out good when you slip up in front of her again."

Benji quit trying to get away from him and instead tried to peer around him. John grunted and moved enough to let Benji and Henry see each other.

Henry's eyebrows raised almost up to his hairline as recognition dawned. John glared, daring him to say anything.

Henry held out one hand. "Henry. I'm John's bestie."

Benji snorted but took Henry's hand. "Benji. And who the hell over the age of thirteen uses the word bestie?"

Henry stood up a little straighter as he pulled his hand back. "Oh ho, the little puppy has a bite."

"You need to leave," John said, thinking he might have to deck Henry.

Benji muttered something John didn't quite hear and he was glad of that. He pointed at Henry. "Out. I'll call you when I don't want to hurt you."

"Might be a while then." But Henry smiled and actually blew Benji a kiss. "You two have fun—and, John?"

John was going to have to kill Henry at this rate.

"I left the condoms I had in my pocket in your bedroom when I came out and saw you two going at it. Figured if you'd had any, they'd be outdated, and I have a bunch more at home. You're on your own for lube."

John had lube, but he wasn't planning on needing it. "Okay, thanks. Leave."

Henry held his hands up. "I'm going, I'm going."

John and Benji moved away from the door, and once Henry was gone and the place locked up again, John kissed Benji again and again.

"You sure about this?" Benji asked him. "I don't want you to regret fucking me."

"I wouldn't, but we aren't doing that anyway," John told him. He kissed Benji until the man was needy, whimpering for him. Then John guided him to the bedroom, where he proceeded to undress first Benji, then himself. "You're so..." *Beautiful*, John wanted to say, but it sounded too intimate a word. "Hot."

"Thanks, you too," Benji uttered as John traced the curvature of his shoulder. Benji was touching him too, but right then John was focused on all the gorgeous skin before him. The dark peaks of Benji's nipples caught his attention and John bent to lick at them.

"Oh, oh, that's..." Benji grabbed a handful of John's hair with one hand and his shoulder with another. "That's so fucking good."

John grinned then went to town, teasing and loving on Benji's nipples. Benji quaked and keened, so perfect it was almost unbearable. John backed him up and laid Benji on the bed. He crawled up and over Benji's body, straddling him, kissing him from chest to chin to lips.

Benji writhed and John reconsidered the whole no fucking Benji thing, at least not yet, but he knew he couldn't do it. He licked Benji's lips then sucked on the bottom one while he plucked at Benji's nipples.

"John," Benji warned, humping air like he was driving in an ass.

"Hold on. Don't come yet."

Benji groaned and closed his eyes. John knew how to get them open.

"I want you to wait to come in my mouth."

"Then you'd better fucking hurry," Benji told him.

John scrambled up and he got off the bed. He saw the condoms on the nightstand. John took two of them, then got back on the bed and kneeled there beside Benji. He held up both condoms. "Are you okay with this?"

"If by *this* you mean sixty-nine, gimme." Benji held out one hand.

John grinned and dropped the rubber onto Benji's palm. "You do yourself, I'll do me, that way I don't have to worry about coming before I get to feel your mouth on my dick."

"Damn," Benji moaned. "Okay. Deal, because otherwise I might come, too."

They each covered their erections, John having trouble paying attention to what he was doing because Benji was so sexy.

When they'd gotten the rubbers on, John maneuvered his way around on the bed until he had his cock aimed at Benji's mouth. Benji's thick shaft was right there, if John curled himself up a little.

Benji shoved at him. "Let me get on top. Works better."

John went over onto his side then onto his back. He spread his legs wide and Benji moved over him. Benji's cock slid right into his mouth, and John thought something short-circuited in his head. He panted for a moment then got Benji's cock in hand.

"Suck me," Benji pleaded.

Like he needed to ask! John opened up and lapped at the fat tip. The latex was awful, but once he slid his mouth down and his jaw ached from the stretch of it, once he felt the thickest vein pulse and smelled Benji's musky scent, John forgot about the taste. He let his eyelids droop and he moaned as he took Benji in deep.

Benji moaned in return, the vibrations shooting from John's cock to his balls. He bobbed up then down again and got his hands on Benji's nuts.

Benji sucked him harder, and he cupped John's balls in his palm. John began to thrust, little movements at first as he made sure Benji could handle it and didn't object.

At the same time, he increased the suction to Benji's cock, and Benji used his free hand to grab John's ass and pull.

John didn't need to be told twice. He pushed in deep, Benji's throat muscles contracting around his crown. John drove in a little more and his eyes ached as pleasure began to flow through him.

His own cock was encased in perfection, heat seeping through the rubber, Benji's mouth working John's shaft.

Benji gave his nuts a little tug and John yelped, but the pain turned from something bad to something that made him damn near giddy. John thrust and thrust, then his balls pulsed and he hissed as he came, pleasure seeping from his pores.

As soon as he was coherent, John rolled onto his back and patted his chest. "Come up here and fuck my face." He put the other pillow behind his head.

Benji was up and on him like a shot. John opened his mouth and let Benji do what he wanted. Deep thrusts, shallow thrusts, Benji tried them all. John kept at his balls, amazed at the way they tightened up.

"G-good," Benji stuttered, eyes rolling back. He moaned and shook as his climax overtook him.

John wished he could taste him, without the nasty taste of the latex, which now seemed to come back nine-fold. But that wasn't possible, so John just enjoyed pleasing his lover.

After Benji stopped coming, and his breathing slowed, John released his soft cock. Benji tugged at him, but there was the matter of the condoms. "Be right back."

John got up and stumbled twice, but he got to the bathroom. He disposed of the used rubber on his cock, then turned the sink spigot on. After wetting a cloth, he turned the water off and went back to his bedroom.

Benji was waiting for him, watching him with guarded eyes.

"I'm not going to profess undying love, Benji, so just relax." John held up the washcloth. "Catch."

"I must not have sucked you right," Benji grumbled. "Otherwise you'd be worshipping at my feet."

John laughed at that. Benji was something else. "Not your feet, but I might be convinced to worship at your dick."

"It is a very nice dick. I'd bend over for it, if I could."

"That's just wrong," John said. "And I know it's possible. I do have Google, after all."

"I think I'll pass on the self-fucking, thanks." Benji cleaned off his cock, folding the condom in the washcloth. "Do I have to get up?"

"Just put it on the floor." John yawned, and his stomach growled. Food could wait. "You want to take a nap?"

Benji looked like he wanted to say yes, his face lighting up, but then he shook his head. "I'd better not. Gramps likes to get out on Saturdays."

"I understand." John was reasonably certain Benji was just ditching him, but that was to be expected. *Especially after the way we both came – hard.*

"Thanks, for understanding," Benji said. "I'll be dressed in no time at all." He picked up his jeans and began putting them on.

John got dressed too, in his jeans and T-shirt from earlier. "No rush, but I understand and remember the rules. I'll see you around."

"You will." Benji kissed his cheek, then he walked out of the door, leaving John with his thoughts.

Chapter Ten

Having Benji pop in for conversation and blow jobs helped John to have a better beginning to his week than he usually did. After being alone for as long as he had been, John was quickly becoming addicted to having company over. Not just any company, but he wouldn't dwell on that. Benji had been clear about what he could handle.

It was still difficult for John to accept that the line was so clearly drawn on their friendship, yet he knew if he wanted any of Benji's time, he had to let the man set the limits.

John told himself that repeatedly. Benji couldn't deal with a relationship, but John found himself wanting more. Yes, Benji had been hurt, but John hadn't done anything wrong. Explaining that to Benji would have to wait. John knew he needed to be patient.

He even thought about skipping the weekly family dinner, but he'd already mentioned to Benji that he went and ate with his family every Wednesday.

Backing out might have made Benji suspect that John had feelings for him other than those of lust and friendship.

John was afraid that was becoming the case. On Wednesday, he dragged Henry to dinner with him, knowing his siblings and parents would pelt Henry with questions instead of him. The trade-off was that John had to deal with Henry asking *him* questions as soon as John picked him up.

"How do you like having a friend with benefits?" Henry asked right off the bat as he got in the truck.

John scowled and waited for Henry to buckle up. "It's not like that."

Henry rolled his eyes. "Okay, so he's not even a friend and it's just sex. How come we never tried that?"

"Because you like guys who treat you like shit and besides that, gross, dude." John shivered and pulled away from the curb. "That'd be like, spiritual incest or something, since you're like a brother to me."

"Spiritual incest?" Henry repeated, cackling for a moment afterwards. "Oh, God, that's interesting terminology there, John. If it matters, I wouldn't want to fuck you, either. And I am trying to get past the whole dating losers shit. Trying not to be a loser myself, either."

"How's that going for you?"

Henry winced. "I think I might be kind of fucked up. This changing yourself shit is hard."

John agreed, completely. "Yeah, it is. I think we do everything we can sometimes to keep from seeing what's wrong with us and what's wrong in our lives."

"This is getting entirely too deep for me."

"Making your head hurt?"

"Yup," Henry muttered. He sat up a little straighter and turned to look at John.

John tried not to twitch. Henry was about to blast him with something—he knew the signs.

"So does Benji bottom all the time, or have you started switching it up finally?"

John groaned, and had he not been driving, he'd have closed his eyes and banged his head on the nearest hard surface. He should have known Henry wouldn't be diverted from talking about sex, and since John was apparently the only one of them getting any…

"I suppose that's another reason you and me wouldn't ever hook up," Henry went on. "I like bottoming, because, God, when a guy's drilling you hard, grunting and sweating as he holds you down and owns you, it's fucking awesome. Being that guy, though, that's fan-fucking-tastic too. I couldn't give topping up."

"We aren't fucking," John muttered. His cheeks went hot and he wondered why he felt embarrassed not to be having anal sex with Benji. Maybe he didn't really want to know that, as it likely had something to do with masculine image and ego and—

"What? Just frotting? Hand jobs?"

John was fairly certain Henry was being obtuse on purpose, leaving out one very important—and enjoyable—form of release. "You know, I don't have to tell you everything."

"Aw, come on. You have to share. It's a best buds' requirement."

"No it's not, ass." John turned onto the exit for the interstate. "And you know what you left out, anyway."

"Blow jobs," Henry crowed. "Blow jobs are as good as sex-sex, better, sometimes. Are you insisting on rubbers?"

"Yeah." John hated those thin layers of latex now because they were a barrier between him and Benji, but they were necessary considering Benji's desire to remain unattached.

"Well, ick. That makes the blow jobs less fun than actual fucking then."

"They're fantastic," John informed him, shooting Henry an arch look. "Better than anything I can remember getting without a condom in the way."

"In the way, huh?" Henry hummed and John ignored him. "Hey, isn't that your fuck bu—uh, Benji?" Henry asked a few minutes later.

John glanced in the direction Henry was pointing and his chest contracted as he spotted Benji's car, with Benji and another man in it.

"Maybe I shouldn't have pointed him out," Henry said quietly. "You don't look happy. You don't look like a guy having a casual fling with someone else."

John tried hard to force his expression into some semblance of neutrality, but damn, he wanted to throw up. *Benji sure isn't wasting any time, is he?* "It's nothing," John got out, though he wasn't even sure what he meant at that point.

"It's something," Henry said quietly, "and if you're feeling things for him other than lust for his hot bod, then you should probably cut him off before you get hurt."

John feared it was too late for that, but as they rode in silence the rest of the way to his folks' house, John couldn't stop thinking about how much more he would be hurt the next time he saw Benji with another man, or worse, what if Benji thought John was as detached as he was, and he began sharing tales of his hook ups with others?

"John…"

Whatever Henry was going to say, John didn't want to hear it. He refused to look at his friend and concentrated on parallel parking the truck between two of his sisters' cars. There were already some of his nieces and nephews in the front yard, hollering and jumping up and down as they waved.

"It seems like the kiddos are glad to see me," Henry said, amusement lightening his voice. "I've missed the monsters."

"You'll get your fill tonight."

"Hey, John."

John sighed and looked at Henry. "What?"

"You might want to try not to look like you're so miserable. I can only do such much to distract your mom, especially." Henry brushed a hand over John's shoulder. "Just try not to think about it, man. You said y'all weren't exclusive or even dating. Is it really such a shock?"

"No." *Yes. I thought he'd realize… Realize what, you idiot? You're the one who needs to realize he means what he said.* John unbuckled, and opened his door. He pushed down his hurt, knowing he had no justification for it. Benji had been quite clear on what he wanted and didn't want. The fear of having his family descend on him like nosy inquisitors—albeit with his best interests in mind—was scary enough to help John get his wounded feelings and damaged pride buried before walking around the truck to the yard.

Henry gave him a faint nod and mouthed, "Well done", then they were bombarded by sticky-handed little munchkins.

"Who gave you guys candy?" John asked, grimacing as Lacey patted his face. They kind of stuck, his skin to her palm, for a second before separating. "Lacey, that's disgusting."

"Uncle Robert gave us cotton candy," she whispered—badly, the kid was just loud no matter what. "He said cuz it de...de...was gone faster so no one would know."

"I like the way your brother thinks," Henry murmured close to John's ear. "Devious, always a plus in my book."

"You need to work on that," John told him. "Come on, Lacey, let's turn the hose on and get y'all's hands washed. Where is Uncle Robert, anyway?"

"He goed in when you got here," George said.

"Smart guy." Henry took George's hand, seemingly uncaring if it was sticky or not. "Come on, I bet we can beat the others to the hose!"

"Yay!"

John grumbled but the race was on, and it was all he could do not to trip over Lacey or Annie, or any of the other little monsters. Their squeals of laughter and the sheer joy that shone in their eyes did a lot to soothe him, and it wasn't too long before John was actively enjoying himself with his family.

Henry kept at his side and stopped him from being grilled too badly. After John had assured his sisters that he was fine and hadn't yet asked anyone out—not a lie, after all—Henry promptly began nattering on about their clothes and John knew he'd owe his friend big-time. Henry hated shopping, but his sisters loved it and they were only too glad to talk about every purchase they had made in their entire lives.

"How are you doing, Stacey?" Henry gestured to her stomach. "I heard you'll be having another little spawn soon."

Stacey snorted and caressed her belly. "Not soon enough. I still have seven more months of misery to go. I really hate being pregnant."

"Then why do it?" Henry asked, confusion causing him to frown.

"Duh, because the end product is so awesome," Stacey told him. "Men. Jeez, apparently it doesn't matter if they're gay or straight, they're still just as ignorant about women as ever."

"Well, if y'all could be consistent for oh, two minutes in your lives, maybe we would get a clue," Henry retorted.

"We are consistent, y'all are just too dense to comprehend—"

"Hey, can we stop the battle of the sexes?" John asked. Stacey wasn't normally so touchy, but having been around his sisters through each of their pregnancies, John knew Stacey in particular could be...moody at best, and outright combative at worst.

"Stacey was just joking." Henry arched an eyebrow at her. "Right?"

"Not really, but if I don't shut up, I bet John will have Mom in here dragging me off by the ear." Stacey crossed her arms over her chest. "Seriously, I love kids. I'd have a dozen if I didn't have to give birth to them."

"You don't. There's always adoption," John pointed out. "That's what I'll probably end up doing some day."

Stacey shook her head. "Nah, not as long as I have working lady parts. Maybe you could find a surrogate. You were a cute kid for the first few years of your life."

"Too expensive." John chose to ignore the insult as he knew Stacey was joking. "I'm going to go say hi to Mom and Dad."

"Me too. It's not safe here." Henry smirked at Stacey, who flipped him off.

"Om! Unca John, Mommy did a bad sign!"

"Shi—shoot," Stacey muttered, rolling her eyes. "That's right, Lacey, I did a bad sign because I got confused. I meant to point at Uncle Henry."

"Ima tell Daddy," Lacey whined.

John snickered and exited the room, heading for the kitchen with Henry behind him. It was in their best interest to clear out before one of them said something that would have Stacey mad at him.

"She's always been prickly when she's got a bun in the oven." Henry chuckled. "Makes me wonder why Mike wanted to go through nine months of that again?"

"There you boys are! Henry, come give me a hug!"

Henry strolled over to John's mom and hugged her. She promptly swatted him on the butt. "Ow!"

"That's for not coming around for so long!"

"Mom, I doubt abusing him is going to make Henry more keen on visiting," John pointed out, but he couldn't stop a laugh from escaping as Henry gave her a wounded look and rubbed his butt cheek.

"Don't smart off to me, John. I have a wooden spoon within reach."

"I can hand it to her if she comes up a bit short," Jane added. "Henry, your butt isn't scrawny, it can handle a few swats."

Henry glowered at her but didn't argue with Jane. She'd held him down once and tickled him until he'd cried uncle, and that had taught him not to mess with her.

John let himself enjoy the time with his family and Henry. Henry, he noticed, lit up around all of them, and he reveled in the attention—even the teasing. It made John feel bad for not making Henry come over sooner. John's family was as close to a family as Henry had, as his own had long ago disowned him.

* * * *

"Maybe we should give that church your mom was talking about a try," Henry said later as John was driving him home. "Sometimes I miss having something to believe in."

John had known Henry forever, it seemed. He hadn't been around his parents much but knew they'd been devout to their religion, to the point of turning their backs on Henry when he'd come out.

"I didn't think you were into all that religious stuff," John muttered as he concentrated on not getting side-swiped by a moron who obviously didn't use his side mirrors or rear-view.

"When have I ever been 'into' religious stuff?" Henry asked. "I'm not. That doesn't mean that I didn't used to believe in God and shit. I just—you know I don't think religion is a good thing. I think believing in something, *that's* a good thing. Maybe keeps a person from feeling so alone in the world."

John wished like hell he wasn't driving, because this sounded like a deeper conversation and it called for more of his attention than he could give. That didn't mean he wouldn't try to understand. "You're not alone, Henry. You've got me and my family —"

"And while I love y'all, none of y'all are there when I can't sleep at night, when I'm alone and wondering why my parents loved me less than their religion, or why I keep picking losers, or why I fucked around on the one decent guy I've dated."

John hadn't heard Henry mention his parents in a long time, but he supposed no one ever really got over being abandoned. It would have killed him if his parents had turned their backs on him.

"I'm not trying to sound ungrateful to you or your family," Henry continued. "It just isn't the same, and I *am* alone a lot of the time. I miss feeling like I'm never alone."

"Do you believe in God?"

"I don't know if there's a god or not," Henry said after a moment. "Or if there is, if he, she or it is anything like the Christian God. Or if the Christian God is anything like the god I had crammed down my throat as a kid. That one was mean and killed off everyone on the planet but one family, you know? I never understood that one. But what if there's more, or if God isn't that vindictive, angry annihilating force? What if God really is just another form of love?"

John shook his head. "I don't know, Henry. That's some pretty deep philosophical stuff right there and I am not the person who'd have answers. Mom and Dad might be able to help you out, or —" John took a breath and forced the rest out. "We can give that church a shot, I guess. Go together this Sunday, if you think it might help you figure out some of those questions."

"Really?" Henry sounded so surprised, John winced. "I know you aren't all into the whole God or religion thing."

"I'm not a rabid atheist," John said dryly. "I respect other people's opinions and beliefs. I guess I just can't fit religion into my beliefs."

"I'm not talking religion. I'm talking believing in something bigger than religion."

John didn't get it at first, then he thought maybe he did. "It's not religion that saves people."

"Nope, and I'm not looking for saving. I'm just—" John heard Henry shuffle his feet on the floorboard before he resumed talking. "I just feel lost, I guess. More than I ever have except for right after the genetics told me I no longer existed for them. I don't want to be that obsessive, that brain-washed. I…"

John waited as Henry sat quietly, and just when he thought Henry was done, he spoke again.

"I don't know what I want, but I'm not happy with myself, and I obviously have problems. Who doesn't? I'd just like to go and see what the church is like."

John bit back the urge to ask Henry about therapy. He'd discovered that it could be a ruse used to fool one's self if a person didn't truly use introspection and try to discover what in them needed to be fixed.

"We can go," John said before he could talk himself out of it. "I'll find out what time they have services, and let you know. You can pick which one works best."

"What time do you think you might hook up with Benji, or will you on Sunday?"

"I've no idea. We don't plan that far ahead." They just…hooked up. "We've only been doing this for a few days, Henry. For all I know, Benji might be done with me already. He certainly wasn't alone in his car." The bitterness that crept into his voice gave away his hurt and anger, but John couldn't help it.

"It was easier when you were numbed by drugs and alcohol, wasn't it?"

John made a questioning noise and Henry explained.

"It was easier not to get hurt, because you didn't care. You could fuck around all the time, but no one touched you. Then you got off the drugs and alcohol, and got some help for depression, but you holed up, so you couldn't be tempted or hurt. Benji got in, though. He's not just a fuck buddy to you."

"It doesn't matter what he is to me, apparently. I know what I am to him, and I have to decide if I can keep on with things the way they are between us. I need to be honest and figure out if there's any chance of something more with him, and if there's not, I think I have to end this—whatever it is he and I are doing." John knew Benji had told him what was what, and John had thought he could deal with it.

"You have to take care of you," Henry murmured.

Yes, John knew that. He also knew he'd never meant it when he'd told Benji he could handle having such a shallow relationship—if it was even a relationship—with him. The fact was, John would have agreed to anything to keep Benji coming around.

Henry was right. Benji was much deeper under John's skin than he'd thought.

Chapter Eleven

Thursday morning, John could hardly bring himself to get out of bed. He was exhausted, and staying up late with the hopes that Benji would drop by — and the fear that he would drop by — had resulted in John being unable to sleep much at all. He had wanted to see Benji, to just talk to him, but he was afraid he wouldn't be able to hold back questioning Benji about where he'd been, and with whom.

Sluggish didn't even cover the way he felt. The bathroom mirror reflected back an image that had him grimacing. There was no way he could hide the bags under his eyes. John settled for soaking a washcloth in cold water and pressing it to the puffy skin until the material began to warm. He did it a few times, then began his workday morning routine.

A shower helped him wake up somewhat, but he still felt weighed down and worn out. *I need coffee, lots and lots of coffee.*

Coffee helped a little, and John managed to eat a piece of toast. He left the apartment and told himself he wasn't disappointed that there wasn't a note from Benji on his floor. There hadn't been any notes since they'd begun messing around. Besides, Benji had his cell phone number. If he'd wanted to speak to John or get him a message, it would have been easily done.

That didn't make him feel any better, as Benji hadn't bothered with him. John told himself to quit being such a whining loser. He needed a good night's sleep. Maybe he'd take Friday off work, just stay at home and sleep until he was rested. He had sick days he could use.

He was off his stride at work, and it frustrated him to the point that he made more errors, calling one client by the wrong name and copying down measurements wrong on an order. Unfortunately, he wasn't the one who caught that mistake. The supplier had called and talked to Mr. Stiles, John's boss, about the odd carpet cuts requested. To top that fiasco off, John had also mixed up the colors he'd ordered.

It was no surprise when Mr. Stiles barked at John to get in his office a few minutes before it was time to go home. John cringed and got up from his desk, feeling the eyes of everyone in the vicinity on him. He tried for about two seconds to keep his head up and his shoulders back, but he just couldn't do it. All he wanted was to go home and hide away for a little while.

"Yes, Mr. Stiles?" John said at the boss's doorway. He knew better than to just walk in.

Mr. Stiles had his head down as he read something on a stack of papers in front of him, but he rolled his eyes up and looked at John. "Come in and shut the door before you sit down. I'll tell you straight off, I want an explanation for today's mistakes. It's not like you to do things like that, and last week, you had problems, too."

John had entered and shut the door as soon as Mr. Stiles had told him to. He strode to the chair in front of the desk and sat while listening.

"Are you using drugs again, John?" Mr. Stiles asked without hesitation.

"No!" John jerked his head up and knew he had to look as startled by the question as he felt. "No, sir, I wouldn't do that again." Mr. Stiles had been so much more supportive about John getting help once John had talked to his boss about his downslide.

Mr. Stiles leaned back in his chair and looked John over critically. "It looks like you have, or else you're hungover. Unless you're sick?"

"I don't feel so hot," John told him, realizing how truthful the words were. "I'm just worn out. Haven't slept as good as I need to. I haven't been doing anything illegal. Henry—he's my best friend—he and I had a few beers on Friday night, but was the first alcohol I'd had in years. Haven't had any since then."

Mr. Stiles tapped the desk with two fingers and John tried not to fidget.

"I think if I could have tomorrow off, just...just get my head together—" John stopped, and Mr. Stiles narrowed his eyes.

"Are you having more problems with depression? Sometimes the medication begins to be ineffective, you get immune, something like that," Mr. Stiles said. "I told you, my sister is bi-polar. The medication she is taking now isn't the same one she was on a few years ago, and that one wasn't the first she'd been on, either. It took her doctor almost a year to find something that would help stabilize her moods. Now we have to wait and see how she does on this new one. It's tough."

John was listening, but he was also thinking about the way depression had snuck up on him before, like a silent, insidious thing that had slowly taken him over until he was almost lost in it.

"You should take tomorrow off, and perhaps call your doctor or psychiatrist, whoever works with you on it and see if they can evaluate you. I don't want to see you continue spiraling downward."

That jerked John out of his thoughts, and he said, "I don't know that I'm spiraling downward. It could just be that I'm tired and things in my personal life are stressing me out."

Mr. Stiles raised an eyebrow in a questioning manner, but when John didn't volunteer any more—and he wouldn't, not under threat of firing, because his private life was his own business. Mr. Stiles eventually quit giving him that look and John sat for another moment, waiting for his boss to speak.

Mr. Stiles sighed and scratched at his wrist, as if something was irritating him there. He glanced at it, then returned his gaze to John. "Take tomorrow off, but I want you in here Monday. Hiding away won't help anything, and I won't let you do that. If you *are* sick on Monday, I'll require a medical note for your absence."

"I'll be here, sir." John stood and leaned over enough to offer Mr. Stiles his hand. "Thank you. I'm truly sorry for messing things up like I did."

"You're a good salesman, John." Mr. Stiles shook his hand then released it. "Go home, get some sleep, and call someone tomorrow if not sooner to see if it's anything more than exhaustion."

"Yes, sir." John left the office. He knew he was lucky to have a decent boss, but he still felt a little irritated over the lecturing on his mental health. John knew how to take care of himself.

Right, dumbass, that's why you didn't catch on to the similarity of the symptoms of a recurrence and your entirely blah feeling until Mr. Stiles brought it up. Genius. John had lived with the knowledge that he'd likely have more episodes of depression. Judging what was just a bad or down mood versus what was a fuckup in his brain chemicals wasn't easy.

It also wasn't something he'd thought he was capable of figuring out on his own. The temptation to just go home and leave off dealing with any of it was great. John stood outside in the parking lot, sweat streaming down his back and brow. He'd left his briefcase in the office, his suit jacket too. Did he want to go back inside? Everyone was probably already gossiping.

John simply didn't have the energy to mess with going back for his briefcase, or the looks he might have gotten. No one was going to steal his briefcase or his jacket. He strode to his truck, eyes stinging as sweat dripped into them. John grabbed the door handle and hissed, letting go of it quickly. He hadn't even unlocked the damned truck.

Once he'd done so, and got in, John started the truck. The blast of cold air made him shiver, and he leaned closer to let it buffet his skin. When he didn't feel like he was going to melt into a puddle of boiled misery, John buckled up and started the drive home.

Except, he couldn't help but think that Dr. Hannah's office was only a few minutes from his work. That was one of the reasons John had picked her, and because he had thought she was a decent doctor.

Walk-ins weren't done, he knew that, but he still found himself taking the exit for the center her office was in. It kept drumming in the back of his mind that he could slip fast and deep into something that might be very hard to crawl out of. He'd told Henry once that functioning through depression could be like trying to swim through setting concrete. Wasn't he feeling close to that now?

John parked at one of several available slots and shut the truck off. He didn't linger, almost afraid he'd have some sort of immediate and intense breakdown. He knew better, rationally, but it didn't matter.

Inside the building, he had to take the stairs up to the fourth floor. Despite the AC, he was sweaty again when he turned the knob on the door to Dr. Hannah's clinic. The receptionist looked up and smiled at him. "Mr. Weston, you aren't due in for a few weeks yet. Is there something I can help you with?"

He noticed that all of the chairs in the waiting room were empty and assumed the office was about to close. John became uncomfortably aware of how he must look, sweaty and breathing a little heavy as the heat had pummeled him. He didn't want the receptionist to think he was having a mental breakdown, so he took a steadying breath and tried to smile. "I'm just wondering if I can leave a message for Dr. Hannah? I was driving by and thought it'd be easy to zip in and ask instead of calling."

Which, he realized, actually made no sense. He could have called and saved himself the heat, the stairs, the embarrassment…

"Actually, let me see if she's available." The receptionist picked up the phone before John could protest.

John wiped his forehead, using his shirt sleeve to soak up the sweat. He then wiped his palms on his pants and walked over to sit in a chair about halfway between the receptionist's area and the door. The receptionist, a nice woman named Juleya, asked if Dr. Hannah had time to see him. She smiled and murmured something he didn't hear, listened for a moment, then hung up the phone.

Juleya smiled at him and stood up. "She'll see you now, if that's okay? I'll run your insurance information after I take you to her office."

John got up and was at the door leading to the back office when Juleya opened it.

"Thank you," he told her. "I just want to make sure I'm not—" He gestured helplessly under her sympathetic gaze.

"It's all right, Mr. Weston. Just come on back and let's see if Dr. Hannah can help you."

"Yes, ma'am. Thank you," John said again. He followed Juleya to the opened doorway.

Dr. Hannah looked up from her notepad. "John, come in. Thank you, Juleya."

John went in and had a seat in his regular spot while Juleya closed the door and left him alone with the doctor.

Dr. Hannah studied him, but she didn't make any comments on his appearance. She picked up her pen and spoke. "What brings you in today, John? Is there anything specific you're concerned about?"

John cleared his throat and nodded. He twined his fingers together in his lap and hoped he didn't sound like a paranoid fool. "I—I've been having some trouble, and I don't even know when it started."

"So you may have been having issues when you were in last week?"

John bit his bottom lip, thinking about the question. His lip throbbed and he let it go. "I think I've had issues all along. I mean, I don't think I've been honest with myself, or you, but not on purpose. I just didn't know some things about myself. But what I mean now is, I'm worried I'm beginning a relapse into a depressive episode."

"We discussed how this might happen," Dr. Hannah said, and when he nodded she continued. "Some people have situational depression, or a chemical imbalance once in their lives, caused by things we haven't yet pinpointed. Then there are people who have a lifelong battle with the disease. There is only so much medication can do, and no one pill is an instant cure. That being said, tell me why you think you are close to or beginning to enter a depressive state."

John told her, haltingly at first, then with more certainty, the reasons he suspected he was in trouble. Talking it out, naming off everything that made him suspicious, helped John in a way he couldn't explain. It was as if speaking somehow made the problems coalesce into puzzle pieces that slid together. He could see where he'd been in what he'd call a brain chemical downer for a while, paddling to keep his head above water. Only it wasn't water, but that wet cement, and he couldn't paddle fast enough.

"You've become sexually active again?" Dr. Hannah asked when John began to tell her about Benji.

"Uh, yes. Yes, as a matter of fact, last week I had a…a hookup, with Benji and another man, too."

Dr. Hannah's eyes widened and her face turned red. John realized what he'd said, and how it must have sounded.

"No, no!" He waved his hands in front of himself. "God, I don't mean the three of us did anything. It was two separate men, two separate occasions, only now it's just Benji and he's not interested in it being just me because his ex screwed around on him and I told him how I used to be."

"Undermining yourself with him?" Dr. Hannah asked in a slightly raspy voice. Her face was still tinted with a blush.

John hadn't intentionally undermined himself with Benji. "I told him before I knew about his ex. I don't know if I would have blurted everything out about me being a slut in the past if I'd known what he'd been through."

"And he's now wanting to be able to have unattached sex with whomever, including you?"

"Yeah, I guess. I mean, he is." John sighed and rubbed at his chest, where a dull ache was trying to kick up. "I don't want him to, and I can't tell him that without losing him completely."

"John, don't you think that perhaps Benji is not in the best frame of mind right now? He sounds very self-centered, and I'm not criticizing his need to be focused on himself, but *you* are my patient, and *you* are the one who is going to be hurt more than you already have been. You want more than what he's willing, or able, to give right now, John. It might be in your best interest to step back and give Benji some space."

"If you lo—" John stopped and shook his head. "I don't love him, but I think I could, and I was going to quote that annoying as hell saying about setting what you love free."

Dr. Hannah grunted, marking something down on the notebook. "That is the most misquoted saying. Or perhaps I should say the most abused. It gives people an excuse to be jerks to others sometimes."

"Is an excuse really necessary?"

"Not at all," Dr. Hannah said with a slight smile on her face. "It would be nice if people truly thought out their actions and words before doing or saying anything, but we're all only human. We screw up a lot."

"We do." John cleared his throat then asked, "So what can I do to get past this roadblock in my life?"

Dr. Hannah took out another pad, one John recognized. "First, but not necessarily the most important, I am going to add another medication to what you're taking. It's been proven to help with depression when taken in conjunction with your current meds. Then, I want you to book another appointment for Monday. We'll do weekly sessions until you and I are both convinced you're doing better."

John wished that were possible. "My insurance won't cover that many visits. The limit is twenty-five visits a year."

"We'll work something out, John. I offer a sliding scale program for patients. Perhaps that will work for you, but don't worry about it right now. We'll deal with it Monday once Juleya has had time to check your insurance versus how many appointments you have left before hitting the twenty-five limit. I'd think it'll be okay for a while yet, and we won't necessarily have weekly appointments through the end of the year."

"Okay." John's tension eased at the possibility of being able to get the help he needed. "It pisses me off.

If this was for diabetes or something, I wouldn't have limited visits."

Dr. Hannah nodded. "It's the stigma, mental illness isn't a true illness. We know better, but the money makers in the insurance business will fight to ever acknowledge that."

John took the prescription from Dr. Hannah. "Thank you."

"You're welcome. And, John?"

He stopped mid-rise from his chair. "Yes, ma'am?"

She watched him with a serious expression. "I want you to think about what we've discussed in regards to Benji. I know you probably want to put him first, but at this point, you need to do like he is and focus on yourself."

Yeah, John didn't like that one bit, but he didn't argue. He wasn't sure what he was going to do in regards to Benji.

John thanked Dr. Hannah again and thanked Juleya as well when he stopped by the desk to set up an appointment on Monday. He had three and a half days before he would be back in front of Dr. Hannah, and he'd need to have some decision about Benji made by then.

Or not. Dr. Hannah won't kick me out of her office if I tell her I'm still letting Benji have his way. She didn't give me a timetable for making any changes, and she didn't demand any, she just suggested.

He had a lot to think about, and while he wanted to get home and see if Benji was interested in hanging, he was equally reluctant to do so. In the truck, John glanced at the prescription. He recognized the name of the medicine as he'd seen commercials for it. With his luck, the shit would kill off his libido. It was a risk and not uncommon side effect of antidepressants.

"You'd think they'd want to make sure something depressing like a limp dick wasn't a side effect," John muttered. "Guess it keeps the drug companies in business." He decided to take the prescription to the Walgreens by his house. Usually it didn't take long for his prescriptions to be filled there and they already had all his insurance information on file.

Half an hour later, after getting stuck in the traffic snarl from hell when everyone had to rubberneck the broken down car on the highway, John made it to Walgreens. It was seven o'clock and he wondered if Benji had plans for the night.

"I have his number, too," John told himself, taking his cell phone from his front pocket. He'd had it on silent and when he looked he saw he'd missed one call from Benji and had two texts from him as well.

John read the texts first, smiling despite his worries over being hurt when he saw that Benji was asking if he was okay since he wasn't home yet.

Then he got irritated because of it. Benji didn't expect him to check in, did he? Okay, he was being a dick. Benji had probably wanted to hook up, and when John hadn't answered his call or show up at home, or respond to texts, Benji might have been concerned. It didn't mean he was checking up on John.

It'd be rude to make him wait any longer if he's worried. But John didn't call, instead he sent a text telling Benji he was late because he'd had an appointment and he'd be a while still.

Benji texted back with a smiley emoticon and asked him if he had plans for the night. John looked at the text. There was his out, but he wasn't willing to take it.

No plans, John replied, and added that he had Friday off, too.

Benji sent another smiley — the man was possibly addicted to the things — and asked that John text him when he got home.

John's dick started to plump up when he read that. "Cut it out," he grumbled. He didn't want to be walking around Walgreens with a boner.

Fortunately, the store wasn't crowded, and there was no line in the pharmacy area. John dropped off his prescription and was told it should be ready in ten to fifteen minutes.

That was good. He wandered the store, picking up a few things while he was there, including more condoms. Better to be overstocked than understocked, that was his new motto. Since he hadn't had dinner, John grabbed a honey bun and a soda. He paid for everything but the medicine then sat down in the pharmacy waiting area and ate his snack.

"Mr. Weston, your prescription is ready."

John stuffed the last bite in his mouth and waved to let the pharmacist know he'd been heard. A gulp of soda helped wash the gooey mess down his throat, then John dusted his hands off and stuck the honey bun wrapper in the nearby trash bin. He paid for his prescription, not surprised when his co-pay was eighty bucks. At least the insurance had covered some of the medicine's cost.

He texted Benji as soon as he was parked and out of the truck at the apartments. It was strange, but he didn't feel lethargic like he had earlier. John put it down to being horny, and he had to admit, the promise of seeing Benji perked him up.

Until he remembered the man in the car with Benji the night before. John slowed his stride as he headed for the complex building. He willed himself not to ask questions or be snarky because he was hurt.

Actually, he decided, the best thing to do was to not talk. If his mouth was otherwise occupied, he couldn't blurt out shit that would possibly scare Benji off.

John hurried up and went inside. He took the stairs at a faster than normal rate, and wasn't surprised when he came out of the stairwell to see Benji leaning against his door, a wicked little smile in place.

John narrowed his eyes and stalked over to Benji. Something like surprise flitted over Benji's face, but it was gone so quickly John wasn't sure he'd really seen it. There was no one else but them in the hallway, and John had to kiss Benji before either of them spoke.

Benji's lips parted and John cupped his nape. A tug had Benji in his arms, then John's mouth was on his, pressing hard as he thrust his tongue against Benji's. John closed his eyes, letting Benji's taste flood his senses.

Benji grabbed at him with both hands, and a sweet, whimpering sound escaped him. John swallowed it eagerly. He dropped the package he'd brought in with him from Walgreens and used that hand to rub Benji's back, all the way down to the swell of his ass.

God, he wanted to fuck Benji, to lose himself in the head and grip of his body. John tried to get closer to Benji, needing more, more of everything about the man. Benji's back hit the door and he grunted. Their kiss turned into a collision of teeth and lips that had John tasting blood. His or Benji's, he didn't know, but it had him pulling back.

"Sorry," he rasped.

Benji just looked at him with wide, stunned eyes.

John took the keys from his pocket and handed them to Benji. "Can you open it?"

Benji bobbed his head and turned to unlock the door. John picked up the bag he'd dropped and watched the flex of Benji's ass as he got the door open and stepped inside.

John followed him in and kicked the door shut with his heel. Images of Benji in the car with another man kept popping into his head and that made John's voice gruffer than he'd intended when he spoke.

"Strip."

Just that one word, but it ratcheted up the sexual tension between then immediately. John hadn't been anything but willing and complacent since they'd started whatever it was they were doing. Tonight he just needed something he couldn't explain. Part of it was some instinctive urge to take Benji, to fuck him until he knew he belonged with John.

That scared the hell out of him. John wasn't going there when he was in such a mood.

Benji was quickly removing his clothes after having hesitated a moment. "Are you finally going to fuck me?" he asked.

Would that keep you from getting fucked by someone else? John didn't want to know the answer as he suspected it'd make him want to put his fist through the nearest wall.

"No, but you'll have something up in your ass."

Benji's cock pulsed at that, and his hands shook as he finished taking his pants off.

John went into his bedroom and got the lube along with a dildo he hadn't used. The lube he tucked in his shirt pocket, but the dildo he held in his hand. He'd thought maybe — but the idea of fucking himself with it had been unappealing. He'd never bottomed, and if he ever did, his first time wouldn't be with a toy.

Carrying his supplies, John returned to his living room. Benji was leaning against the couch with his legs spread while he was stroking his cock. His balls hung heavy between his thighs.

John walked up to him and rubbed the dildo over Benji's nuts.

"Nice," Benji hissed, and John bent to lap at one of his nipples.

Benji made a strangled sound. He left off masturbating and instead grabbed at John's hair to pull him closer.

John kept rubbing the dildo over Benji's sac, while at the same time licking and biting his nipple. He used his free hand to pinch and twist the other nipple. The little buds were quickly swollen, hot, and hard as stone peaks. John worked them in a rougher manner and Benji shouted, pushing him away.

John opened his mouth to apologize, his stomach plummeting as he realized in his aggression he'd hurt Benji.

But Benji was whimpering and squeezing his dick with enough force the head was darkening rapidly to a purple color. "Almost...came," Benji said between panted breaths.

John looked at the abused tits, the tips so pointed and swollen. The skin was almost raw, but Benji had liked it, had almost come just from John playing with his nipples. Why hadn't he checked to see if Benji liked nipple play before then?

Not wanting to lose any of the heat arcing between them, John brushed the back of his fingers over one of

Benji's nipples. Benji shuddered and whimpered. John liked both reactions, a lot.

Benji's lips parted, and John was on them like a starved man finding a feast. He plundered Benji's mouth, claiming every bit of it he could taste. Benji moaned for him and John pulled back enough to spin him around. He had Benji bent over the couch in a second and was rutting against his upturned ass.

"Please, please, please, fuck me," Benji begged, undulating beautifully. John shifted his stance so his dick lined up in Benji's crease perfectly. He was glad he'd left his clothes on, otherwise he might not remember his own restrictions. Benji's ass was plump with a light trail of fuzz going down his crack. John was going to lick his way down it someday, and taste Benji's ass, just rim him until Benji came and came and came.

Tonight, he was going to take Benji, but with the dildo he still had rather than his own cock. The dildo wasn't super long, at about six and a half inches, but it had a nice girth to it.

Benji was still pleading, his want so big he was shaking. John stopped enjoying himself so much and he took the lube from his pocket.

"Patience," he growled at Benji. Benji went up on his toes, wiggling his ass. "Be still or you'll make me drop this dildo, then we'll both have to wait while I wash it and dry it off."

"Ugh!" Benji stilled then turned his head just enough that John could see him frown, like not moving was the worst thing in the world.

John set the dildo on Benji's back and poured lube on it, then poured more at the top of his crack. After he popped the lid down on the lube, John tossed it aside. He rubbed Benji's ass cheeks, squeezing them and enjoying the fleshy feel of them. The dildo wobbled and began to topple off, but John caught it. "Almost had to take a break," he teased.

"Fucker." Benji shook for him and John ran two fingers down his slick crease to the ringed muscle nestled between his cheeks. "Oh," Benji sighed when John began rubbing over his anus. "Guh, that feels so goooooood."

John slipped one finger in easily, the heat and tight grip of Benji's body something to behold. John bit back a moan as he pushed his finger in deep. Benji cursed and John withdrew, then pumped two digits into Benji's ass.

"More," Benji demanded.

John thrust faster and twisted his fingers around. He brushed over Benji's prostate and got a keening sound out of him. "Like that, do you?"

"Y-yes." Benji rode his fingers for several minutes, then John worked a third one in. Benji felt so deliciously snug, John knew he'd die if he ever did decide to fuck him. He sped up his movements, slamming in deep and fast, caressing Benji's gland every third or so thrust.

John contemplated a fourth finger, or… *Oh God, fisting Benji's ass, making him mine, holding him, filling him —*

But fisting wasn't something he'd ever done, that he knew of, and he wouldn't do it without a great deal of discussion and research. Instead he pulled his fingers out, and before Benji could bitch about it, John slammed the dildo home.

"Fuck!" Benji shrieked and arched like a taut bowstring. John didn't hesitate. Benji was ready to be fucked.

"Going to," John told him, then he followed through, fucking Benji with the dildo as Benji gasped and begged for more. John gave it to him, driving the toy in with more force, and Benji shoved a hand beneath himself. He jerked his cock while John held one of his ass cheeks aside and plowed his hole until Benji shook and cursed as he came.

He was beautiful—his muscles rippling, sweat making his skin gleam, his ass clenching and releasing, that tight hole of his trying to hold the dildo in place. John ached to come so bad he felt like one throbbing nerve.

As soon as Benji came down from his climax, John carefully removed the dildo and dropped it on the floor. He unfastened his pants and shoved a still-lubed hand past the waistband of his underwear. His cock was so hard, so wet from pre-cum leaking out.

John got his hand around his shaft and eyed Benji's ass. It'd feel so good to ride his slick, warm crease until he shot all over Benji's back. But that would probably be too much like a commitment to Benji.

"Do it. Put that huge fucker in me," Benji urged. "There's condoms—"

"No. I want—" John traced Benji's crease with his fingertips.

Benji craned his neck and his sloe-eyed look almost had John coming where he stood. "Do it," Benji urged. "You can come on my ass even. Just let me feel you somewhere on me."

That last bit was said in what sounded like a plea to John. He didn't wait to find out. He got his pants and underwear down past his ass. There was still lube all over Benji's crack and some on his back too from when John had poured it on the dildo. John scooped up the lubricant and coated his cock with it. He leaned over Benji a little, fitting his cock in Benji's crease.

"Oh fuck," he rasped, folding himself fully over Benji. The friction was wonderful, Benji—everything about him perfect like this. John thrust and almost sobbed at the relief of being able to do so. He hooked his arms beneath Benji, under his chest and crossed so he grabbed the opposite shoulders. Then he set about coming and easing the need that pounded through him.

John let that need take him, let it shoot from his balls to his cock then out to his hips as he rode Benji. Sensually filthy words spilled from Benji, daring him, begging him, cursing him. It drove John past the point of reason with arousal. He curled his fingers against Benji's shoulders and grunted and gasped.

Benji tipped his hips up and bumped against him. John's orgasm hit him like a freight train, stunning him, knocking him for a loop as he jetted spunk between them.

"That was...something else," Benji said minutes later, when John started to move again. This time, he wasn't trying to get off, just up so he could wipe them both clean before they got stuck together. "You should do me like that more often," Benji continued. "I didn't know I'd like that whole bossy attitude thing, but it was hot."

Great, he'd probably just given Benji another way to play with whoever he fucked next.

Chapter Twelve

It was a good thing Benji hadn't spent the night, John decided the next morning. For a little while, John had thought Benji was going to keep snoozing away on the couch, but about an hour after John had fucked him with the dildo, Benji had woken up and come after John like a leopard stalking its prey. Benji had sucked John off, teasing him and driving him wild.

John kept thinking of how much more intense it'd feel without the rubber on, but he'd clenched his jaw to keep from saying so. Benji had beat off at the same time and left his spunk splattered on John's feet and carpet. Shortly after that, Benji had left.

There'd been little to no conversation, and John had been good with that. No, he was resigned to it. John had showered and taken his new prescription meds along with his usual one.

And slept like the dead. He'd felt like someone being resurrected the next morning. His limbs and body were weighed down with a sleepiness he knew was drug-induced.

Great. I'll be a zombie for weeks until I get used to the shit. John had been through it before. Once his body got used to the medicine, it wouldn't hit him so hard. But God, he'd be useless all day.

John rolled over on the bed and forced one eye open so he could see the clock. When he did, his other eye shot open and he shoved himself up.

"The fuck," he mumbled, rubbing his eyes. There was no way it was almost noon. Except it was, he discovered when he looked again. His cell phone confirmed it. John saw no missed anything on his phone and decided he'd just lie in bed a little while longer.

Hours later, his bladder was threatening to explode and kill him. John didn't think death by bladder tantrum was a very fun way to die—like dying would ever be fun—so he forced himself to get up and hit the head. *Might as well get cleaned up while I'm in here.*

John took a long shower, and he didn't beat off like he'd normally do. Whether it was the medication or the fact that he'd come hard twice last night, he didn't know. He yawned and stretched and started to feel a little more alive by the time he was clean.

John shut the water off and got out. He toweled himself dry and ran the comb through his hair. After deodorizing his pits and brushing his teeth, John proclaimed himself as good as he was going to get and went to get dressed.

The clock beside his bed showed it to be ten past three in the afternoon. John's head felt a bit stuffy, an oversleep headache, something he hadn't had in ages.

Coffee would help. Coffee helped everything. He took his laptop with him to the kitchen.

After setting his laptop down, John put the coffee on then sat at the table. He got the laptop up and online and started Googling for the church his mother had mentioned. He'd come to a conclusion, despite his sluggish day. It was time to start figuring out what he wanted, and taking his life seriously, taking control of his life, instead of just stumbling along, going whichever way he was bumped in.

The church had a nice website, he noted, and several different service times. He bookmarked the page and got up to get some coffee. An hour later, he'd thoroughly examined the entire website and he had to admit it seemed like a decent enough place for a church. John checked the time. *Just after four. Henry won't be off work yet.* He emailed Henry the information.

John sighed and played around online until close to seven. It didn't slip his notice that he hadn't heard from Benji all day. So far, he'd let Benji initiate the hook ups, but he was done being led around. He wasn't looking to get laid, but he did send Benji a text asking how he was doing. Benji didn't text back for ten minutes, then his one word reply of 'okay' came through.

Whether it was wishful thinking or not, John couldn't help but feel like something had happened between them last night. Not the sex, though fuck if that hadn't been the hottest thing he'd ever done, using the dildo on Benji then rutting away on that fine, fine ass of his. The sex had played a part in it, but the emotions — Benji had given part of himself over to John for safe-keeping, if only for the time John had taken control.

It'd been humbling, to be trusted in such a way, and the more John thought of it, the more worried he became that Benji would realize what he'd done and take off. Trust was something Benji didn't want to give, even if it was just of his body, not his heart.

John sighed and rubbed the back of his neck, tension creeping up his spine. It was a Friday night — didn't most sexually active, horny guys go looking to get laid on Friday nights? John used to, and on Saturdays, Sundays, Mondays, all the way through to the next Friday. Occasionally he'd needed a day off the partying scene to get some sleep. John didn't know how he'd done it. Just thinking about it made him tired.

Henry called him close to eight and asked if he wanted to go to the Sunday evening service. The six o'clock starting time would work better for him, so John agreed.

"Have you eaten yet?" Henry asked him.

"Just toast and coffee. New meds," he mumbled, then Henry began pelting him with questions.

"I'm just going to come over. I'll bring Chinese food and crash on the couch since it doesn't sound like you're expecting other company."

John wasn't expecting Benji, and that made him want to crawl back into bed. He wouldn't give in to the impulse. "Fine. Make sure you get some hot oil."

"Ick. How can you stand that shit? It's just hot grease."

"Is not, and you're just a wuss who can't stand a little heat."

"I save the heat for the important stuff," Henry told him.

John chuckled and they ended the call. He supposed it was better for him not to be alone. Henry would talk him into a coma and keep John from thinking too much about what Benji was doing.

* * * *

The weekend passed with John not seeing Benji except for once in the lobby when Benji was taking Mr. Marks out for Saturday shopping. Benji hadn't been able to look at him, and that had hurt, but John thought he'd covered it well. At least Benji had replied to the text John had sent him Sunday morning, asking again if he was okay. He wouldn't push beyond that point.

The new medication was still dragging him down a bit, but he didn't feel the mental fog he'd been experiencing. It was a different kind of weariness and hard to pinpoint. John kept himself busy when he wasn't dozing, catching up on sleep and letting the new meds take him down for bits of time. He cleaned the place like he only usually did before his mom came over, and he caught up on some of the reading he'd intended to do sooner.

Sunday afternoon, he picked out and discarded one outfit after another before finally deciding on dark blue slacks and a short-sleeved, pale yellow polo shirt. He primped a little, then laughed at himself. Even if he tried, he couldn't pretend he was interested in meeting another man. Benji had him hooked, and there was nothing he could do but hope to get through being dumped as a sexual partner without doing something pathetic, like groveling for another chance.

John had more pride than that. He wanted a healthy, loving relationship. He wasn't likely to get that from Benji. Church didn't have to be somewhere he went for a hook up, either. Even as a non-believer, using a place of worship to find men seemed wrong.

But he could go and support Henry, and try to understand his best friend's needs. John was honestly worried about Henry. Maybe this would help him.

Maybe it'll help us both. John almost laughed at the thought. He'd tried medication, therapy, life changes—sort of—and why would he think church would help anything after all of that? He was doing okay, anyway.

John tidied up his bathroom countertop, wiping up the water he'd splashed along with some whiskers from when he'd shaved. He checked himself in the mirror—*still plain looking*—and left the small room. His bedroom was neat, the bed actually made for once. John was tempted to take pictures and send them to his mom, along with the comment, 'Aren't you proud of me?' That was just a little too needy for praise on his part as far as he was concerned.

When John came out of the stairwell onto the first floor, he heard Benji's laugh before he saw the man. Benji sounded happy, not like he was forcing it, and that in turn made John's stomach flip and dip as he feared a run in with Benji and another man. It wasn't until he saw Benji walking with Mr. Marks and Mrs. Royal that John felt like he could breathe without having to curse.

Benji was dressed casually, and the elderly couple were holding hands, looking as if they'd fallen for each other deeply. John's heart ached—he wanted that, the way Mr. Marks and Mrs. Royal looked at each other, as if they were one another's world.

John forced himself to move, to head to the exit. He pasted on a smile, nervous about how Benji would greet him. He'd missed Benji all weekend.

"Oh, John, dear, you are dressed up to go out. You look very dashing," Mrs. Royal said, spotting him first.

Mr. Marks and Benji turned toward him as well. Mr. Marks smiled but Benji frowned deeply, the edges of his mouth pulling down.

"Thank you, Mrs. Royal. You look lovely this afternoon, as usual." John nodded at Mr. Marks. "Good afternoon, sir. Benji."

John wanted to ask Benji what was wrong, but he was afraid to. If Benji didn't want to see him, or speak to him, John would rather not know that until he absolutely couldn't escape the knowledge.

"Do you have a date?"

John blinked, taken back by Benji's question. Well, the question and the tone, because Benji sounded almost...angry. The pinched expression was also kind of a giveaway to John that Benji wasn't a happy man.

"I—" Was Benji jealous? No, that couldn't be. John was just reading more into Benji's words and expression than he should have.

"Why, Benji Marks, you have no reason to be scowling like that," Mrs. Royal chided. "You'll be wrinkled like me in no time if you continue."

Benji blinked and sputtered for a few seconds before he turned and strode off. John gawped at him, confused.

"I do think our plan is working," Mr. Marks murmured.

John didn't ask—everything in him was telling him to go after Benji. Should he listen? John wasn't certain he could trust his internal emotional compass.

"Go after him," Mrs. Royal urged. "Why are you still here?"

"Uh..." John didn't have a quick answer. He took off, his longer stride catching him up to Benji by Mr. Marks' door.

"Benji, wait," John said as Benji shoved a key in the lock.

"Not now," Benji grunted back at him.

Benji had liked it well enough when John had taken over Thursday night. Maybe he should try growing a pair outside of a sexual situation. "Yes, now."

The words had Benji sucking in a sharp breath and stilling his hand on the doorknob. John expected to get blasted for being a domineering jerk, but Benji closed his eyes and shuddered as he sucked on his bottom lip.

He presented such an erotic scene that John wanted to fuck him right there against the door and keep fucking him until Benji admitted he cared for John. Because he did, John could see that now, but whether Benji would let that affect his desire to be free and easy, John hadn't a clue.

"You know, I like you all growly," Benji said after a moment. He peeked out of one eye at John. "What are you doing to me?"

"Nothing," John replied. "Nothing besides chasing you to tell you I'm only going to church with Henry."

"It doesn't matter to me," Benji told him, but he averted his gaze by closing his eyes again. "You're free to do whatever and whoever you want, right? I don't get a say in it any more than you get a say in that part of my life—or any part of my life."

John watched Benji closely. "Which is exactly how you want it." *There!* The flinch was subtle but unmissable, as he was looking so closely for a reaction.

"Yeah, sure." Benji opened his eyes again but didn't look at John. "So. Church. That's cool, I guess."

John moved the few feet necessary to bridge the physical gap between them. The emotional one was much larger and more difficult to navigate. At the same time, Benji turned and leaned against the door. He had pinned one of his hands between his lower back and the hard surface, but his other fluttered almost like a bird until he pressed it to his throat as he stared at John with big, fathomless eyes.

John leaned against Benji while he cupped Benji's jaw with his right hand and one of Benji's hips with the left. Then he slowly lowered his mouth to Benji's, watching those dark eyes until his vision blurred and Benji's lids drooped shut. So did John's, and less than a second later his lips were on Benji's, parting them as John slid his tongue inside to tease Benji's.

The moan that left Benji sounded as if it were torn from the core of him. He shivered and jerked his arm free from behind him. Benji grabbed onto John like he feared John would leave him. John in turn feared that he'd never be able to do such a thing. That could be very bad for him and his heart.

Then John quit worrying about it all and just let himself feel. Benji was hard and warm beneath him, growing desperate and writhing as he became more aggressive. John wasn't giving up the lead. He tightened his grip on Benji and held him in place as he ravaged Benji's mouth. John's cock was erect and ready for action, but there was no possibility of any out in the hallway.

Or so he thought, until Benji hooked one leg up around John's hip and began rutting mindlessly, all need and urgency and lack of rhythm. That hungry desperation was irresistible. John moved the hand he had on Benji's hip around to his ass instead. He traced the seam of Benji's jeans with his fingers while diving deeper into the kiss. When he found the hot little spot he'd sought, John pressed hard with his fingers, rubbing Benji's hole through the layers of clothes.

Benji jerked his head back on a gasp, and John opened his eyes just in time to see Benji's roll back as he grunted and came, face slack, lips wet and parted. As badly as John wanted to come, too, he held himself back. Benji needed something from him, and while John wasn't sure quite what that was, he did think part of it was the control that had turned Benji on so much. And, John didn't want to have to change clothes, not when he was already going to be pushing it to be on time.

Benji slumped against the door and unwound his leg from around John's hips. John held onto him, making sure Benji was steady on his feet. Once he knew Benji wasn't going to fall over, John tipped Benji's head up for a soft kiss, the kind of which he'd never shared with him before. It showed his emotions, he feared, but was unable to deny himself or Benji the tenderness.

"I've got to go, but I'd like to talk about—" John bit back 'us' and quickly used, "everything that's going on, tonight if possible."

Benji started to nod then stopped halfway through the motion. "Can't. I've got an interview with the manager at Starbucks." His eyes gleamed and he smirked. "Isn't that where Shane met you the other day?"

John couldn't help being surprised at the hint of threat in Benji's voice. "What does that have to do with anything?"

Benji's smile turned wicked. "Oh, nothing."

John had the feeling that Shane might be getting some nasty coffee if Benji ever waited on him.

"I know it's not the best job in the world," Benji was saying. "But the museums here in San Antonio aren't hiring, and I need a job."

John pulled himself out of his thoughts and replied, "There's nothing wrong with it. I'm just a salesperson. Not exactly glamorous, at all."

Benji pursed his lips then shrugged. "Well, whatever pays the bills."

"Exactly." John took another kiss, putting a bit more force into so that Benji had a nice, melty look to him when John was done. "I'll see you Monday, then." *No more letting Benji run the show.*

"'Kay, unless I get hired and have to work," Benji muttered. "I'll let you know if that happens."

"Thank you." John rubbed his thumb over Benji's swollen bottom lip, them pressed on the center of it. He glanced down at the wet spot on Benji's groin and his own cock twitched. Too bad, because he wasn't going to get any relief for a while. "You look good like this." John didn't explain that he meant pliant and sated, because Benji would likely turn prickly as a porcupine, so instead he left Benji there with a wink and a smile.

John hoped no one would pay attention to the semi-hard-on he was sporting as he strode to the exit. Luckily the lobby was empty except for Shane. John barely acknowledged the man's hungry look, waving at him and heading out of the doors.

His phone dinged and John took it out of his pocket, along with his keys. He read the text from Henry when he stopped beside his truck.

On your way yet?

John smiled. Yes, he finally was on his way.

Chapter Thirteen

The church was bigger than John had expected, even after seeing pictures online. He knew well enough that Photoshopping could create places that appeared more appealing virtually than in reality. That wasn't the case with the God's Love church.

The building itself appeared to be an architect's fantasy come to fruition, with a very modern design. Sharp angles, varying roof heights as well as dozens of windows framed with intricate trim...the church was impressive.

"Love the steps," Henry murmured, and John had to agree. The steps leading up to the church were as wide as the building itself, and they came out in a curvature that looked to be almost flowing as they glinted bronze under the sun.

"Crowded, too," John pointed out as he looked for a place to park. There had to be at least a hundred cars there, maybe more. "Who knew," he murmured, more to himself than to Henry.

Henry picked up on it anyway. "Yeah, well, I bet there's a bunch of people like me who feel lost. When society tells you you're wrong, an abomination and shouldn't have rights like everyone else, it makes you question everything."

"It's getting better. The fact that this church is even here is proof of that." John had to believe it, too, otherwise life would be too depressing even with his medications. No one wanted to be hated and shunned.

"Yeah, I guess. We could always move to a different state, or country." Henry snorted. "Your mom would skin me for even saying that."

"She would. None of her babies can move away."

Henry didn't say anything else and John feared he was thinking about how his own parents didn't care where he was. John couldn't imagine that. He found a parking spot in the ass-end of the lot and shortly after they were walking toward the church. Several people greeted them, nothing too intense, just *hi* and *welcome*. It was weird, but John...liked it, and Henry was smiling in a way John hadn't seen him do for a while.

The steps were gorgeous, and numerous. "By the time we get to the top and find a seat inside, we'll be too tired to stay awake during the sermon," John told Henry.

"No kidding."

To the side of the open double doors, greeters stood welcoming people, chatting, shaking hands and offering hugs. When John and Henry went through, they were stopped by a pretty, bubbly young man who beamed at them like they were something special.

"Welcome to God's Love! I'm Assistant Pastor Luke Aames. Y'all are visiting with us for the first time?"

Since Luke held out his hand, John shook it, but the man's enthusiasm was kind of…it was just too much for John, especially as his adrenaline from the earlier encounter with Benji had crashed by then. John was feeling tired, more so than he should have from the stairs, and he wondered which chemical—his brain or the meds—was fucking with his system.

"Nice to meet you," Henry was saying, and by then John had left off the hand shaking. Henry had a familiar expression on, and John barely kept from groaning. There was a definite predatory light in Henry's eyes.

John stood there, trying not to get in anyone's way, while Henry and Luke made small talk. Finally he shifted his weight to one hip and propped his shoulder on the frame behind Luke.

Henry gave him a startled look, like he'd forgotten John was even there. *That's good for my ego.*

"We'd better get inside. I'm really looking forward to the service," Henry practically oozed.

John loved Henry, but the man could be borderline smarmy at times.

"Hitting on a man of God? Seriously?" John hissed in Henry's ear as they walked toward two empty seats.

"Why not? He was receptive, and maybe I need a holy man to keep me in line."

John glared at Henry. "You need to keep yourself in line. No one else is—"

"Calm down and don't get your self-righteous boxers in a bunch," Henry snapped.

John shut his mouth and thought about what he'd been saying. He *did* sound like a self-righteous, judgmental prick. "Sorry."

Henry grunted and they took their seats, garnering a few odd looks. John knew some people had likely overheard their conversation, but there wasn't anything he could do about it now.

The service began a few minutes later, and John found himself pleasantly surprised. The songs sung by the congregation along with the pastor and assistant pastor were a mix of familiar and new to him. The enthusiasm the people sang with was impressive and warming in a way he hadn't been expecting.

After singing and praying, a sermon was given. It wasn't like the ones he remembered as a kid, with the preacher going red in the face as he hollered for the Lord. No, Pastor Avery, as he introduced himself, spoke in a soothing, strong voice. He conveyed more with his tone than John had ever heard from any other preacher.

And what John got out of the sermon was love — that he was loved, and deserved to be loved. He should open himself and love others, treat them well and use care with every word and deed. Had he heard similar sermons before? Well, he had, but the delivery was so different, it seemed to him new lessons spelled out from the pulpit.

John hadn't come looking for a man, or for saving, but he found himself feeling lighter, and thinking he'd come back, maybe with Benji. *I'd like that, a lot. But first, I'd better keep Henry from making this place his hunting ground, starting with one certain assistant pastor.*

When the service ended after a few more songs and a short prayer, John hooked his arm through Henry's. "This was nice," he admitted.

"It was." Henry sighed and John guided him slowly down the aisle toward the doors. "It was very nice, and I feel like maybe there's some hope in the world. Guess that means no screwing that up with my—" Henry cut himself off and coughed. "With my libido."

"Good plan. I'd like to bring Benji."

"Henry," a friendly, entirely too ebullient voice called out right before they got out of the door.

Henry gave him an 'I tried to be good' look and a shrug. They stopped, tucking themselves into an alcove as members of the congregation shuffled past. One stepped over to join them. Luke smiled as if he'd been given the best treasure ever.

"Henry!" Luke nodded at John. "John, how'd y'all like our service?"

"It was nice," John said, while Henry commented, "It made me feel less hopeless."

Oh, that did it for Luke. His eyes widened and his lips rounded into an O.

Henry grunted like he tended to do when he was uncomfortable emotionally, then he shifted from foot to foot.

"Could I—" Luke began, then he cleared his throat and he glanced at John. "Could I speak with Henry for a moment?"

Henry didn't protest, so John figured he was fine with it. "Okay. I'll just wait out by the car."

"Thanks," Luke said, rolling up onto his toes and grinning brightly again.

God, maybe he's the kind of man Henry needs after all. Surely not even Henry could stand to kill that kind of happiness.

John walked outside and promptly bumped into another man. "Sorry," he muttered, looking up into the rough-hewn face of an older guy. Blue eyes glinted down at him and John felt a fissure of unease. For some reason, an image of Shane flashed through his head.

"It's okay. I don't mind having a handsome young man try to get close to me."

John barely kept back a frown at the cheesy pickup attempt. He shook his head. "It was an accident, I assure you."

"Right. That's all right then, I just thought—" The man shrugged.

John kind of felt bad for him, and remembering the sermon he smiled. "I'm sure you're a nice guy and all, but there's someone I'm hoping to convince to give me a shot."

That got him a smile in return that was neither creepy nor seductive. "I can understand that. Good luck. I'm Dez, by the way."

"John." They stood and chatted for a few minutes, then Henry came outside.

"Let's go."

John frowned at Henry's abruptness and Dez raised both eyebrows up in surprise at the sharp tone. "Sorry," John told him. "I'd better see what's gotten him all bent out of shape."

John jogged down the steps after Henry, who seemed determined to get to the truck before John. If John hadn't been in decent shape, it might have worked, but as it was, John caught Henry by the arm about ten feet past the steps. "What the hell, Henry?"

Henry shook his head and jerked his arm out of John's grasp. "Lemme go."

John wasn't going to force Henry to tell him anything anymore than he'd hold Henry's arm if Henry didn't want him to. "Fine, but if you're planning on pouting I'll make you ride in the truck bed."

"That's illegal," Henry snapped.

"So's being a dick." *Or it should be. We'd have to build a hell of a lot more jails though.*

"Is not." Henry stopped and looked at him. "He turned me down, but offered to counsel me. What the fuck does that even mean, counsel? I don't fucking get it." Henry flung his hands up.

John figured it meant Pastor Luke was smarter than he'd given the man credit for. He didn't think that was what Henry wanted to hear, though. "I think he wants to help you with some of the problems you've been having. The bad decisions with men, feeling lost. That kind of stuff."

"Like I'd go to him for help with any of that." Henry glanced down at the asphalt.

"Why wouldn't you?"

Henry didn't look up. "'Cause he's— I—"

"Take a deep breath and try to answer honestly," John advised.

Henry blew out a frustrated sound. He shoved his hands into his hair and rolled his eyes. "Urgh! Because he'll never like me if he knows me! There, are you fucking happy?"

A group of people walking past looked at them and John tried his best to smile like he didn't want to holler at them to mind their own business. Henry was being loud, after all.

"No, I'm not happy, and you aren't happy, and maybe you should consider whether or not you'd want to be with someone who wouldn't like you if they knew you, Henry. That's just kind of screwed up."

Henry reverted back to his grunting acknowledgments and John kept in a sigh as he started for the truck.

The drive to Henry's was tense, but more because Henry was locked into an inner turmoil and John couldn't help him. When he pulled up to the curb at Henry's place, John touched Henry's arm as he was fixing to get out. Henry met his eyes. "You aren't a horrible person, Henry. Anyone would be lucky to be with you, if you'll just have some faith in yourself."

Henry snorted and opened the truck door. "One church sermon and you start preaching." He got out and slammed the door hard enough to rock the vehicle.

John didn't see any point in getting mad about it. Instead he felt tired and borderline despondent as he watched Henry walk off.

That feeling stayed with him as he drove home and on into the evening. John sat on the couch in his shorts and stared unseeingly at the TV. Nothing was on as usual, and anyway, his thoughts were preoccupied with Benji. He needed to have an actual conversation with Benji, like they'd had in the courtyard that day. John had told Benji about being a reformed slut, but he'd never told him the reason behind those actions, the desperate need to escape from his own head.

Would it make any difference? Benji's like I was, trying to get away from the pain by fucking around. Different kind of pain, but still.

Then again, maybe Benji was just celebrating his freedom after having been monogamous for so long.

They needed to talk, that was all there was to it.

John just couldn't find the right words to text Benji asking him to come over and talk. He wondered if Benji was maybe off with someone else after having come from humping against John earlier. That would fit Benji's pattern—experience something he couldn't control, then off he'd run to find some dumb guy he could handle.

That wasn't fair. John didn't know who Benji was hooking up with, whether the guys were fools or master players. It didn't matter, he supposed, just like it didn't matter that it hurt him. Benji had somehow become important to him, maybe partially because of the similarities John saw in them. But Benji was also the kind of person who just shone with an inner light, though he seemed to try to snuff it out.

John didn't want that to happen. There was enough bad shit, bad people in the world. People like Benji, and even Pastor Luke, they radiated a core of goodness. Now, maybe Benji's didn't shine so bright, but John would bet, given the love and comfort Benji craved—whether he'd admit it or not—Benji would be a beacon of joy for anyone around him.

Oh God, he'd be one of those constantly happy people…

For some reason, that made John grin so widely his cheeks hurt.

Thinking about Benji made John's cock twitch, but he didn't get an erection. He'd had one earlier, sure enough, when Benji had been getting off on him, but the meds tended to make things…soft, and erections more difficult.

On the other hand, he'd probably have awesome stamina once he did get hard.

John groaned and thumbed his cell phone again. Why was it so hard to just send a fucking text?

Benji responded well to John being firm with him. John frowned. Had Benji and Derek been in a relationship like that, with Derek being the dominant of the two? Was that why Benji had let Derek kiss him like that in the lobby?

John's temper pricked thinking of the kiss, of Derek touching Benji after having hurt him. He opened up his texts and didn't let himself think about anything more than spelling out *Come over if you're done with the interview* before hitting send. The worst that could happen was Benji would say no.

Or tell me he's busy with another guy, that would suck pretty hard. John got up and went into the bathroom. He washed his face off and patted it dry. He looked okay, he guessed.

John kicked off his sweatpants then pulled on a pair of jeans and a tank top just as a knock sounded at his door.

John's heartbeat kicked up. It couldn't be anyone other than Benji. *Unless Henry came over, or Shane – God, if it's Shane I might punch him. So not the guy I want to see.* If it was Henry, he'd try to be a bit nicer.

But it was Benji, standing there, chewing his thumbnail and looking sweet and nervous. Seeing Benji like that calmed something in John.

Wordlessly, John held the door open to let Benji in. Benji continued gnawing on his thumbnail as he walked past John and headed to the living room.

"Kitchen," John said, more because he didn't think Benji wanted anything easy right then. He could be wrong. Benji would let him know if he was—throw a fit, holler, storm off. Yeah, Benji would speak up somehow, which would mean Benji didn't like the total domination thing. Maybe he just got off on it sexually.

They really needed to learn more about each other.

"How was church?" Benji asked as he took a seat at the table.

"It was good. How did the interview go?" John walked to the fridge and opened it up. "You want water or soda?"

"Uh." Benji turned and looked in the refrigerator. "Eh, I don't really like that kind of pop, so water. Interview was okay, I guess. I have to go back for a second interview on Tuesday with the GM."

"You never said anything about not liking that brand of soda before." John took out two bottles of water and handed one to Benji.

"Well, usually I'm fucked out one way or the other."

"Yeah. Do you think you'll get the job?"

Benji shrugged. "Hard to tell. I hope so. I don't like living off of Grandpa."

John sat and opened his bottle before taking a long drink. He wasn't sure where to begin, but figured as much as there was unknown between them, anywhere would do. "I never told you why I screwed around so much before."

Benji eyed him suspiciously and picked at his thumbnail again. "No, but I didn't ask."

Not sure if that was a hint or not, John decided he'd just talk, and if Benji didn't want him to, then eventually Benji would tell him to shut up.

John took another drink first, because he was nervous about telling Benji he was mentally ill. Those two words had so much stigma attached to them… John sighed quietly and set the bottle down. He made himself look right at Benji. "Here's the thing. There are words, labels, that can be used as weapons against you, sometimes even by yourself."

Benji frowned and stopped messing with his thumb. "I know I've been screwing around but most guys do—"

"I'm talking about me, Benji," John said, trying to keep his hands from trembling. He could feel them tensing, feel his muscles quivering deep inside his arms. John clenched his hands into fists. "I meant what I did, which yeah, lots of guys do. I'm not Derek, I won't cheat on you. Yes, I was promiscuous before. I just, I needed—" God, his chest ached and his left temple throbbed. "I didn't know what was wrong with me, just that when I was having sex, I didn't have to think or feel, really. Not any of my feelings, anyway. But to be wanted, to have guys bending over for me like they couldn't give it to me quick enough—that fed this empty spot I had. Temporarily."

Benji wasn't frowning now—he was scowling. "How is you telling me that you fucked every goddamned guy you came across supposed to make me—" Benji huffed and flung his hands out on the table, smacking it hard. "What the fuck is it you're trying to do, John? If you don't want to have sex with me anymore, just say so!"

"That's not it. I want you to understand why I did what I did, then *you* might not want to have sex with *me* anymore!"

Benji leaned back and gave him a cautious look. "If you're fixing to tell me you're positive, I gotta say, you should have said so sooner—"

"That's not it, either, Benji. I swear I'm not. I told you, I've had tests and tests because yeah, I was careless, I don't even know how careless. I was high, I was drunk, and I didn't care if I lived or died." John took a deep breath and let it out. "I think I wanted to die, most of the time, but I was too chicken to flat-out kill myself."

"What the fuck, John?" Benji was back to scowling at him. "Why would you want to die, and especially from

AIDS or some other disease? Even AIDS is treatable for most people, they can live long lives with it, but there's syphilis and shit that doesn't do anything but bitch slap antibiotics aside. Even when I was in Mexico fucking around, it was condoms for anal. Okay, not oral, I already told you I like sucking dick without rubbers. Doesn't mean I swallowed often."

The chance for transmission through oral was small if there were no open wounds in the mouth or anywhere else the sperm landed, but it was still there. John wasn't going to point it out, because he knew Benji was aware of that from the belligerent tilt to Benji's chin.

"I didn't care what happened to me, and believe me, I know how lucky I am," John told him. "I've had acquaintances who had unprotected sex once and that was all, just once, and they were positive because of it. We know the risks, the stories, but that doesn't make us use protection does it? Not all of us, just like straight people don't, and they know what can happen, too."

"Right, so I still don't get it." Benji arched one eyebrow at him. "What are you trying to say?"

John hitched a shoulder in response to that look. "I have a depressive disorder. I spiraled way downward before anyone figured it out. Sometimes I still have bad days, and the meds I'm on aren't a cure. I just got prescribed another one to help, since I've been feeling like I'm slogging through hip-deep mud." He forced his gaze up to Benji's. "So I'm mentally ill, and while there've been celebrities coming out and talking about it more and more, it's still… It still sucks, and people think as soon as they hear mentally ill, that I'm crazy, or if they hear the word depression, they think it's emo shit. I had my grandma ask me what I had to be depressed about. Like I chose to be that way." He shrugged, averting his gaze since Benji was just watching him. "Like anyone would want to be that miserable. I don't think she ever had any respect for me after that. She died thinking I was just pouting or being a drama queen, if she even thought of me at all."

The silence stretched taut between them for several minutes. John's breathing became shakier, his lungs not quite managing to take in enough air. He shifted in his seat, his ass going numb on the hard surface. How could Benji be so still?

"I don't know much about depression," Benji began slowly, yet his voice still startled John into looking over at him. "I admit, depression and mentally ill seem like two different things to me, but I get that's my ignorance, and my labeling and stigmatizing and all that. I think mentally ill, it's like those people you see on TV who are raving at the air and shit, but I do know that's just me not thinking. I know, too, in case you're wondering, that Derek was just a cheating whore. I think I knew it before we ever went out, but I was young and dumb and idealistic, and I chased him like I'd never had an ounce of pride. I practically had to beg him to fuck me and pop my cherry."

John wanted to go back and beat the shit out of Derek for being such a dick. Benji had a faraway look to his expression as he continued talking.

"Once he did, I felt like I'd won a prize, you know?" Benji snorted. "The Corpus Christi player was going to be mine. I don't know why I wanted him so bad. I just did. Maybe because he didn't want me. I just kept following him around and it was probably awesome for his ego. Eventually he fucked me again. Then again, and about the fourth time or so, I just didn't go home — moved right in without an invite, but Derek didn't seem to mind. We always used condoms for anal sex, but that was all we used them for. Guess I got in the habit of being careless." Benji sucked in his bottom lip then let it go. "What are we doing here? Why are we talking instead of fucking?"

"Because I want you to know I'm not Derek, I'm not like him." Among other things he wanted Benji to understand.

"Okay, I get you saying that. Time will tell though, huh?"

"Benji, you're the one doing all the screwing around," John couldn't help but snap. He dropped his head in his hands. "Sorry."

"You're jealous?"

John dared to peek at Benji, who had a surprised look on his face. "Yeah. I'm sorry. You told me, just sex, no strings, but it's more than just fucking to me. I like what I know of you. I want to know more. I want to be able to talk to you about my day, listen about yours, learn new things every day—"

Benji sat up straight and pointed at him. "That...you're talking about a relationship."

"Yes. I want to be more than just another guy you're getting off with," John confessed. "I saw you, Wednesday night. You were with another guy in your car. I... I wanted to beat the shit out of whoever was going to be with you. I don't want to share anymore, Benji."

Benji went back to biting at his thumbnail, eyeing John almost cautiously. John searched for something else to say, but though he knew there were many issues to bring up, none of them were currently popping up in his mind.

He took another drink, draining the bottle and setting it on the table afterwards. Benji was still eying him, but this time there was something hot and needy in his eyes. John told himself not to give in until they'd hashed some of the stuff out between them.

"You want to fuck?" Benji asked, as if reading John's mind. John started to answer but Benji held up one finger. "Because I'm hard as hell, and really, there's nothing I'm going to be able to concentrate on until I come."

Chapter Fourteen

John gestured toward his groin. "The medicine can make it difficult—" he began, but Benji slid from his chair onto the floor. He crawled over to John, stealing John's breath with the sensuous way he moved.

"Let me worry about that," Benji purred, pushing John's knees farther apart. John's gasp filled his lungs when Benji put his warm mouth right over the tip of John's denim-covered dick. "Mmmm."

The vibrations from that little hum seemed to shoot right down to John's asshole. He clenched everything from his abs down as a want he wasn't familiar with came over him.

Benji looked up at him with an eagerness that spread lust through John like lava flowing free from a volcano. John put one hand on Benji's shoulder and fisted the other in his hair. He pulled Benji closer and was rewarded with a scrape of teeth over denim that made his nuts ache for release.

Benji began licking and nipping along the length of John's cock. John guided him, holding Benji by the hair. When he tugged a little, Benji's eyelids drooped and he moaned, spreading more pleasant vibrations through John.

John gulped when Benji nudged farther down to John's balls. Benji opened his mouth wide and breathed, sending wet heat through the material and onto John's delicate skin.

Then Benji moved down more, and though he couldn't get to John's hole, he let it be known he wanted to. John scooted to the edge of the chair, his heart thumping heavily.

Benji pushed one of John's legs up and John got the picture. He put his heel on the table and gave Benji some room. Benji looked up at him.

"Do it," John rasped, feeling like his entire body was one raw, wavering nerve.

Benji dipped his head and began doing something — John couldn't see, exactly. It felt so good though, wet and warm and occasional pressure against his pucker. Not too much, not too rough, nothing that would scare John off from enjoying what was being done.

Benji moaned and ran his hand over John's cock, bringing it to almost fully erect. He canted his hips a little, all that he dared lest he fall out of the chair. Benji angled his head and John suddenly felt more pressure against his hole.

His cock pulsed, and John rubbed his free hand over it, urging himself to get fully hard. Benji made a sound that sounded a growl and a whimper combined, garnering the response from John's cock John had been working on.

Benji pulled out a condom from somewhere, John hadn't a clue where he'd kept it. Just one second Benji was eating his ass through his clothing and the next he was sitting up on his knees waving the rubber at him.

"Fuck me, John."

John didn't argue. He lowered his foot down from the table and stood on shaky legs. "Come to my bedroom," he said as he held a hand out to Benji.

Benji put the condom package in John's hand but pulled himself up when he did it. John closed his hand around Benji's, wanting the comfort of Benji's hand in his. Benji didn't pull away either and actually sidled up close to him. Their arms and hips bumped as they walked, and John liked it very much.

"The guy in the car the other night, that was Mr. Ruiz' grandson. Grandpa asked me to give him a ride home instead of making him ride the bus." Benji sounded embarrassed to confess that he hadn't been hooking up with the guy. "George—that's the guy's name—he's straight. He also didn't want to be in the car with me once he had the nerve to ask if I was a 'fag' and I went off on him."

John stopped them in the hallway and tipped Benji's chin up with two fingers. "He could have hurt you."

Benji gave him an arch look. "And you know that how? I can take care of myself, John. I'd have pulled the car over and beat the bigotry right out of his nappy ass if I'd needed to."

There was so much fire and spark in Benji's voice, John found himself believing that yes, the man could take care of himself in such a situation. Still… "Well, if you could beat the bigotry out of him, then for all mankind's sake…"

Benji snickered and turned his head aside. "Right. You know what I meant."

"I do." John nudged his bedroom door open. He stopped Benji and kissed him then, a solidly thorough kiss that left Benji clinging to him. John pushed back a hank of hair from close to Benji's eyes then kissed him again for good measure.

Without a word spoken between them, he led Benji into the bedroom. John began kissing him again with every step, the kisses lasting longer and longer until they were moving together, legs in synchronicity.

They reached the bed and John had Benji down on the mattress, pressing him deep into it as John plundered his mouth. Benji had the sweetest mouth, but then, everything about the man appealed to John—everything but the promiscuity.

John kissed Benji until soft whimpering sounds spilled from him, then he began kissing his way down Benji's body. He exposed skin along the way, unbuttoning Benji's shirt, plucking at his nipples then twisting them. Benji bucked and moaned, a sound John was becoming addicted to hearing.

He spread the shirt open, not bothering to push it off. John left marks all down Benji's torso.

"Raise your hips up," he rasped when he tugged on the waistband of Benji's jeans. He was wearing a faded, loose pair, not the painted-on, tight ones John had gotten used to seeing him in.

Benji tucked his ass up and John slid his hand down the front of Benji's pants, covering that thick cock of his. With his other hand, he pulled on the jeans. Benji wiggled and pushed at them with his hands too, and they had him naked but for the shirt still barely on him in a couple of minutes.

John licked Benji's balls, sucked them until they were drawn up tight in their sac. He thought of the precautions he'd insisted on and what he wanted to do. John licked behind Benji's nuts to his perineum and Benji yelped at the same time he clamped his legs together, creating a vice around John's head.

"What're you doing?" Benji squealed.

John pulled at Benji's legs until he loosened them. "Tryin' to breathe." Benji's leg muscles weren't lacking.

"Sorry, but I thought you were going to…"

John used his thumbs to spread Benji's cheeks and expose that little hole. "Just a little."

"But—"

"You can say no," John told him sincerely. "Or you can let me just…lick."

God, it sounded so dirty when he actually said it. John's cock couldn't get any harder and Benji shook for him like he was close to coming.

That was, as far as John could tell, a yes. He dipped his head down and ran the flat of his tongue over Benji's hole.

"Oh my God!" Benji shouted, digging his heels into the mattress. John grinned and licked again, this time tracing the clenching ring with the tip of his tongue. He'd love to just dive in, to push his tongue into the heat of Benji's body, but he didn't. He licked and loved on that little ring until Benji was babbling incoherently, undulating on the bed. Only then did John stop—

And wonder what had happened to the rubber. It'd be easier to just grab a new one from his bedside table. John patted Benji's hole with his fingertips. "Let me get the stuff so I can fuck you."

Benji muttered something unintelligible, and John grinned as he got up. He shucked his own clothes in record time, then got the lube and a condom. Benji started to roll over, and John stopped him. "No. Face to face, for now at least."

Benji's eyes widened and his breath sped up a bit. John opened the condom package and plucked out the rubber, letting the empty packaging fall. He rolled the latex down his dick.

After lubing his cock and his fingers, John knelt on the bed and began massaging Benji's hole. He rubbed and rubbed on his anus until it loosened up enough to easily take his finger in.

"More," Benji demanded immediately. John pinched the inside of Benji's left thigh. "Ouch! Oh my God! Don't do that unless you want me to squirt out a load!"

John chuckled and pushed a second digit inside Benji's ass.

Benji went back to making nonsensical noises as John loosened him up. He brushed over Benji's prostate and Benji howled while he wrapped a fist tightly around his dick. "John," he panted repeatedly.

John was good with two fingers. He withdrew them and crawled up between Benji's legs. "Open your eyes," he said.

Benji blinked a few times then focused on John. "Please."

John dipped his head down and licked Benji's lips. At the same time, he began pushing with his hips. He had to jostle the bed and Benji a bit, because his cock wasn't lined up like he'd thought and that hadn't been Benji's ass hole he'd poked at. John got his cock in hand and the tip pressed to Benji's pucker.

"Relax," he urged, then he was sinking his cock into the fiery heat of Benji's body.

Benji wailed and grasped one-handedly at John. John got his hand around Benji's wrist and pinned him in place. He lowered himself enough that he could dip his head down and mark up Benji's pretty skin.

"Don't come yet," he warned Benji, "because I'm not anywhere close. I'll fuck you through your climax, fuck you until you're hard again, then fuck you through round two. Even then, I probably won't have come yet." He'd make sure Benji got a fucking that'd keep him satisfied for days.

"Sounds…" Benji panted, "perfect."

John pushed his cock in until he was buried to the root. He gyrated a little, just experiencing the gripping muscles and intense heat. Benji's hole clenched tightly around the base of John's dick. It was an incredible feeling. John gave a little thrust and Benji moaned.

He kissed Benji then, slowly, in case Benji wanted to object since John had just been licking his ass. Benji ran his tongue over his lips and John took that for the offer it was. He pressed their lips together and withdrew his cock a few inches.

Benji scrambled to hold onto him, finally gripping at John's upper arms. He slammed back in, and Benji keened, need ringing in his voice. John kept at it, fucking Benji deep, hard and slow. The way Benji's inner walls gripped him, rippled around him, was marvelous.

John kept his weight on his elbows and forearms, dipping his head for open-mouthed kisses. Benji's lips were parted as he panted, his eyes almost closed, a glazed look in the part of them John could see. The kissing was mostly one-sided, with Benji lost in pleasure but occasionally finding enough cognizance to flick his tongue against John's, or nip it.

He shifted until he had each of Benji's wrists pinned beside Benji's head. When he slid back in, John pressed his belly down to grind against Benji's cock. It wouldn't be enough to get Benji off, probably, but it would drive him so close to the edge he'd teeter there for a while.

Benji whimpered and he wound his legs tightly around John's hips. John grinned against Benji's lips. The grip Benji had on him restricted his movements, but driving into Benji with wicked little jabs was making them both crazy.

John thrust and thrust until he was light-headed from everything — the controlled movement, the feel of Benji around him, under him, the sounds he made and the blissful look on his slack features.

It was not enough, for either of them, though. "Let go," John growled, and Benji took a minute but he got his legs unwound from John's waist.

John withdrew his cock from Benji's ass and before Benji could do more than gasp, he rolled Benji to his side. John pushed Benji's top leg up, spreading his ass and exposing his glistening hole. "Beautiful, baby," he murmured as Benji grabbed at his raised leg.

Bracing one hand beside Benji's shoulder, John guided his cock back into the welcoming heat of Benji's body. The way Benji arched his back and the clamp of his ass around John's dick was maddeningly amazing.

John drove in slowly until he was fully seated, then he began thrusting, slowly at first, but as Benji's breath hitched and moans spilled from his lips, John's control began to shatter.

He dropped down over Benji and began hammering his ass. Each thrust added to the building euphoria until sparks danced in front of John's eyes. Benji mewled and got his hand on his cock. When he began jacking himself, John started fucking him harder.

"Yes," Benji hissed, and a second later his eyes shot wide open as he threw his head back. John felt it immediately, the tight, tight constriction around his cock as Benji's climax began. "Ungh—"

John shivered and nudged his cock in just a little deeper then held still while Benji came. As soon as Benji was done, John kissed him again. It wasn't the best kiss, the most comfortable one ever, but the tenderness in it melted John inside.

He pulled out carefully and was still erect. "On your back," he urged as he tugged the condom off. John dropped it on the floor as he knelt, knees right on the outside of Benji's hips. John began beating off, staring at Benji's belly and chest, wanting to mark that fine honey skin with cum.

"Oh," Benji panted, excitement in his voice. John darted a glance a little higher up and saw Benji grinning like he'd never been so happy before in his life. Benji got a hand on John's balls, and John wasn't lasting long after that. He jerked himself off roughly, needing more sensation than it'd normally take, then he was coming, his balls pulsing cum up to his cock.

When the first jet of spunk splattered on Benji's chest, John shouted, unable to contain the possessiveness he felt. Benji was his, and he wouldn't give the man up. Anything more complicated to think about than that would have to wait.

John pumped three more streams of cum onto Benji then scooted down. Benji released his nuts, and he began licking up his own semen. He'd rather have tasted Benji's, but until they were committed to each other and tested, he'd have to settle for this.

"Oh my fucking hell," Benji rasped. He petted John's hair.

John knew it was pretty erotic to watch someone lick cum up, either their own or their partner's. At least, it was to him, and Benji sure seemed to like it too.

"John…" Benji began, only to yelp when John licked his belly button. "Ticklish! Stop!"

As it wasn't his aim to torture Benji, John left off the exploration of his belly button and finished licking the last stream of spunk.

"Come here," Benji urged, tugging on his hair.

John let himself be guided up the length of Benji's body. He met Benji, eye to eye, hovering above the small man on the bed. *Is this where Benji runs again?* John's pulse fluttered, nerves jangling inside him. "Don't leave. Don't run off again."

Benji jerked his head back against the pillow as if John had slapped him. A hurt look flitted over his face. "I guess I deserved that."

"I didn't mean it as an insult," John began to explain. "I want—I need—something more than just fucking, and I want it with you, Benji. I won't hurt you, not like Derek did, not at all if I can help it."

Benji averted his gaze and let go of John's hair.

"Benji, it'll get old, the fucking around with nameless guys and sleeping alone—"

"I know," Benji admitted quietly. "It already has."

John was stunned by the admission, and he couldn't think of a word to say. 'I told you so' was completely off the list of possibilities. John settled instead on kissing the slight down-turn off Benji's lips. He slid his tongue into the moist cavern of Benji's mouth, licking and savoring Benji's taste.

Benji relaxed beneath him, shuddering once or twice, his cock firming up a little. Still, he didn't capitulate when the kiss ended. Benji sighed and closed his eyes as if he were satiated and sleepy. "Can I think about it, please? I don't want to jump into anything after the way I did with Derek."

"You aren't chasing me, here. I'm chasing you," John couldn't help but point out. He touched Benji's lips with his fingers. "But take the time you need. I want you sure."

Benji pried one eye open and looked at him. "What about the depression? Is that going to be an excuse to cheat?"

John shook his head so vehemently he thought he might have rattled something upstairs. "No. No, it won't be. Before, I just didn't know—I was using drugs, sex and alcohol to mask it all. I didn't know I had anything wrong with me. Robert, my big brother, I accidentally called him one night and he came over." John repressed a shiver at the memory. "I was a mess, and he was pissed off, to put it mildly. But, here's the thing. One of my sisters has depressive disorder too, and Robert had seen her break down before her diagnosis. He saw similarities someone else might not have, and he bullied me into getting help. I owe him for that, and I won't fuck everything up after he put so much effort into dragging me out of the pit. All of my family did."

Benji opened his other eye. "All of them?"

"My immediate family, yeah. They're great." He wanted Benji to meet them, but blurting that out seemed a good way to spook him. "Mom and Dad, they've been together since high school. All of my siblings, they're married and have kids." John was the only one left who hadn't found the person he'd spend forever with. No, that wasn't right. He'd found him, now he just had to convince Benji.

"So you get all the nagging?" Benji asked.

John grinned and eased onto his side, lying close to Benji. "Nah, not too much. They want me happy, and you know how it is. Married people want everyone married so they can share the misery," John teased.

"No shit. My folks never married each other. Mom had me while she was still in high school. I was kind of shuffled between her house and my grandparents." Benji rolled onto his side and propped his head up on his hand. "When Grandma Marks died, that was like losing my mom, you know? She'd been the one who raised me for the most part. I don't hardly ever see my mom now, or talk to her. She has a whole 'nother family to dote on. I think she doesn't like to be reminded of her mistake."

"You're not a mistake," John said instantly.

Benji laughed bitterly and rolled his eyes. "Oh yes I am. That's okay. I know she didn't want me. She kept up an act around people, played like she gave a damn, but trust me, she was so distant when it was just us, there was no way I could fool myself." Benji took a deep breath and blew it out gustily. It sent the hair dangling on his brow fluffing up in the air. "I'm okay with it, I mean it. She was young, dumb, and obviously full of —"

"Gross," John interrupted. "I get it."

Benji beamed at him, obviously pleased at squicking John out. "Right. So she was an idiot and didn't practice safe sex — one of those careless heteros, huh? Anyway, I don't know my dad. Mom didn't list him on the birth certificate, and she used to give me a different name

211

every time I asked. I don't know if she participated in a gang bang or is just fucking with my head."

"That's...awful. Your grandparents didn't know if there was anyone in particular she was hanging out with?"

"Nah. She was a beach bum. She'd hang out with a big group of kids on the beach all the time. When she got pregnant, she quit leaving the house except for school, grandpa said. They never pushed her for a name, and she never offered one. When I started asking as a kid, I swear it was like a game to her, trying to see how many names she could come up with."

"How could she not think you'd believe she was a slut?" John couldn't comprehend such carelessness.

"I don't think she cared." Benji closed his eyes and put his head down. He curled up against John. "This kind of means I might be willing to try."

John was so stunned he couldn't reply at first. That was what Benji meant by talking to him about his past. He was willing to give more than just his body. It was enough, for now, and John was going to tell Benji so, except Benji snored softly and cuddled in closer, and John knew he didn't have anything more important to do then than hold Benji while he slept.

Chapter Fifteen

John's fear that Benji would dart away from him upon waking didn't come to fruition.

Benji stretched and did something very close to purring before he yawned so big his jaw popped. "Ow," he mumbled, opening his eyes. "You're still here."

John was tempted to say the same thing, but didn't think he could get it out without sounding relieved that Benji hadn't hauled ass. He didn't want Benji to know how much he had begun worrying already that Benji would back out on giving their relationship a shot.

"I was wondering if you'd like a midnight snack." John's rumbling stomach had woken him up. Work tomorrow would be fun, with him being awake now, but that was okay. He had Benji here.

"I am kinda hungry," Benji admitted. He rolled over and rubbed his eyes. "Man, what time is it? Is it really midnight?"

"Yeah, it's a quarter after, actually." John sat up and swung his legs around until he had his feet on the floor. "Grilled cheese okay?"

"Aw, God, that sounds soooooooo good! How do you make them?" Benji bounced somehow—John was sitting on the bed and he was jostled as Benji made his way to sit beside him. "You don't use mayo or anything disgusting like that, do you?"

"Ack, no. That's blasphemy." John mock-shuddered. "Butter, the real kind, and two slices of cheese, American and Swiss or provolone, your choice."

Benji scrunched up his face and poked his bottom lip out. "I can't have all three?"

"You can have anything you want," John said quietly, meaning it in every way.

Benji stopped pouting and looked at him with so much surprise, and something else, something John thought might be longing. "Two is just fine, your choice," Benji replied just as softly, and John wondered if he was reading more into the offer than Benji intended. He didn't think so. Benji was reaffirming his earlier desire to have a relationship with John.

"Okay then. I'll make us both one of each kind." John took a quick peck on the lips and stood. "You can shower if you want, or go back to sleep—whatever, make yourself comfortable."

"Shower sounds great." Benji's voice cracked on the last word and John looked back at him. Benji held his hands up. "What? You've got a fine ass. Keep walking that way."

John felt himself blush, and a check of his chest showed it to be blotchy pink. He headed for his sweats.

"Don't get dressed on my account," Benji told him.

John snickered and picked up his favorite pair. "I'd rather not burn anything important."

"That would be a shame."

"You can borrow some pants or PJs if you want. They're in the second drawer." John pulled his pair on, trying not to laugh as Benji whistled and harassed him. Once he was covered, Benji gave an exaggerated groan of disappointment then told him to go be a good boy and cook. John flipped him off.

"Later, if you're up to it."

John was sure Benji didn't mean it as a dig, but whether or not he could get hard was a sensitive subject for John just then. He told himself not to be so thin-skinned.

In the kitchen, he laid out the supplies he needed to make the grilled cheeses. The shower came on in the bathroom, so he figured Benji was rinsing off. John began whistling, putting the sandwiches together and feeling happier than he could remember being for some time.

Benji came in just as John was pouring them some orange juice. "You okay with juice? I found a can in the freezer."

Benji frowned at the pitcher. "They still make frozen juices?"

"Uh, yeah," John said, barely keeping from rolling his eyes. "Haven't you seen them in the grocery stores?"

"Uh, no," Benji scoffed, mimicking him. "I don't look for them so I don't see them. Heh. I used to like to pop the lid off the cans and eat the concentrated goo. It was like a push-up pop without the push-up part."

John laughed and sat down. Benji joined him at the table. "So you're saying it was like eating a sherbet?"

Benji snapped his fingers. "That's what it's called! I couldn't for the life of me remember. These look divine." He picked up a grilled cheese. "And yeah, I'm good with OJ. Love it, actually." Benji took a bite and his eyes closed as he moaned. "S' good," he said around a mouthful of sandwich.

"Thanks." John began eating his, not worried about manners when his stomach was gnawing on his back bone. They made casual conversation after inhaling their first sandwiches, then John almost choked when Benji slid his foot up John's thigh.

"Think you can go another round, or do you need to get to sleep?" Benji asked, toeing John's balls.

John's cock was waking up, and John decided thinking positive was better than worrying. "Sleep is overrated."

* * * *

Monday morning, John awoke feeling alert and...happy, despite the lack of sleep. Surprised, too, because Benji was still snoring away in his bed. John brushed a kiss over Benji's forehead, then he got up and began his usual morning workday routine.

He hummed, something he hardly ever did, but it was like the joy inside him couldn't be contained and had to seep out in some kind of sound. John found himself grinning and hoping, things he'd not thought to be doing on a Monday morning, ever.

In his bedroom, Benji was still sleeping, sprawled over the queen-sized mattress like he was trying to claim every inch of it. John smiled at the image he made, then he dressed quietly, sneaking peeks at Benji all the while.

In the kitchen, he made his coffee and toast. He sat down to eat and write Benji a short note, telling him to make himself at home and that he hoped to see him this evening.

John took one more look at the adorable man before leaving.

He really liked having Benji there.

* * * *

Work was typical Monday drama-trauma-shit, with customers ranting and employees snapping. John took a few minutes to talk to Mr. Stiles and let him know that he was doing better. He also thanked his boss for being patient with him. By the end of the day, he was tired, but the thought of seeing Benji energized him.

Considering Benji had sent him more than a few raunchy texts during the day, John also wasn't concerned about being able to get and retain an erection. He'd been half hard on and off all day, thanks to the naughty messages.

It was a good day, with Benji spending another night with him after a round of fucking that left them both exhausted. Tuesday was almost as good, but Benji was late getting to John's place because of the interview.

Wednesday, John reluctantly went to his parents' without Benji. John had hemmed and hawed about asking him, but when he'd finally gotten the balls to do it, Benji had looked at him and shook his head. "I'm sorry. Not yet, okay?"

John hadn't been able to argue with him. Benji had the right to take it slow if he wanted.

Their week together passed quickly. Benji was waiting for John when he got back from his folks' place, and Benji slept over every night but Friday as he had to be up early to take his grandpa and Mrs. Royal to a slew of yard sales.

"The early bird gets the worm," Benji had said, rolling his eyes. "I'm not a fucking bird and neither are they. Gramps can't possibly fit one more piece of junk in his place."

"Maybe it's for Mrs. Royal," John had suggested. Benji had given him a calculated look.

Saturday morning at six-thirty, John was awoken by someone pounding on his door.

"Benji, you shit," he growled when he looked through the peephole and saw Benji beaming at him. "You evil, evil shit." But John's stomach was all fluttery, and he was smiling fit to model toothpaste when he opened the door.

"Didn't want to be the only young'un on the yard sale trip," Benji explained, handing over a cup of hot coffee.

Sunday was a surprise, with Henry asking John to attend church services again. Benji refused to go, and John felt slighted despite himself at being turned down twice in the span of a week. He did his best to hide it, though, and promised Benji an intense evening when he got home.

John couldn't quite bury his hurt, but he didn't want to bring it up, either. He didn't want to risk an argument or anything that might set Benji off him. Their fucking was intense that night, with John rougher, leaving marks—love bites and just bite-bites—on Benji's skin. Benji loved it, whimpering and moaning when John fucked him so hard his hip bones left bruises on Benji's ass.

Later, in the middle of the night when John couldn't sleep, he thought he'd puke when he'd realized he'd let anger push him, not affection. He'd poured his anger and hurt into Benji's body through harsh thrusts and stinging bites.

John was ashamed of himself. Guilt pressed into him, curdling the food in his stomach and making him have to run for the toilet. He didn't want to puke on the floor or the bed, and he didn't want to wake Benji up.

John retched until his stomach was empty, then he dry-heaved until tears streamed down his face and his stomach muscles burned horribly. He rolled his forehead over his arm, then slowly got to his feet. He wobbled, weak and worn, but took the time to flush the nasty stuff down. After washing his face off and brushing his teeth, John felt no better than before. Benji had enjoyed what John had done to him, but if he'd known the anger behind John's roughness...

It was too much. John couldn't look at himself in the mirror. He didn't deserve to lie beside Benji either, so he wrapped a towel around his hips and went to flop on the couch. Hours later, he watched the sunlight creep through the cracks around the blinds. John rubbed at his eyes and debated calling in sick. He didn't feel like going to work, and for once, he wished his darkened mood was the result of his chemical imbalance, but it wasn't.

Guilt, plain and simple, was eating at him. John knew he'd fucked up, and it was worse, in a way, that Benji didn't seem to have been aware of it. Twice now John had taken Benji like that, although this last time had been much rougher. Would he lose his temper someday and seriously hurt Benji, if this was how he reacted to feeling slighted?

No, I'll never hurt him. If he'd told me to stop, or said I was hurting him, I would have quit doing what I'd been doing last night. John felt the truth of that in his bones, and it eased his guilt a little, but not enough.

He'd talk to Benji tonight and explain how he felt rejected. Twice he'd asked for Benji's company, and Benji had said no. Yet John had gone with him to the yard sale trek, and even to Mr. Marks' for dinner Saturday evening. All he wanted was for Benji to be willing to extend their relationship out in John's direction, toward his family and interests.

Because, for one thing, John's family meant the world to him, and he knew they'd adore Benji. Benji needed that as much as John's family needed to see him happy.

And secondly, John thought he liked the church services and people there. Sure, Henry was a scowling, snarly thing and still refusing to let Pastor Luke counsel him. That was kind of entertaining to watch for a few minutes, then it just made John sad for Henry. Henry still wanted to go to church, too. John wasn't sure if it was for the services or for Pastor Luke. Henry wasn't saying.

But John wanted Benji to be a part of *his* life. He didn't think he was rushing, since Benji was bringing John to dinner with Grandpa.

John got ready for work, not cutting himself a break and calling in. He chugged too much coffee and damn near sprang a bladder leak by the time he got to work, and the rest of the day proceeded in true Monday fashion. It sucked, and John got his ass chewed by a customer and Mr. Stiles after the customer called the boss, apparently not satisfied with reaming John. John hadn't done anything wrong except order the colors and designs the man wanted.

Unfortunately, the customer was claiming differently. When John showed Mr. Stiles the signed order forms approving the carpet colors and designs, Mr. Stiles calmed down a little. He said he believed John, but the customer was insisting he hadn't picked those products and that he'd signed a blank form. There wasn't much they could do really to prove otherwise, and the company would have to eat the loss, all because an asshole had changed his mind.

John left work feeling worse than when he'd arrived, something he wouldn't have thought possible. Benji's cheery texts had only added to the guilt, especially when Benji had been oohing and ahhing over bruises and other marks on his body.

To be fair, Benji sounded happy about being marked. John wanted to bang his head against a wall to knock the guilt out. If Benji enjoyed it, why should he feel guilty? John went around and around with his thoughts until finally he was ready to punch something — not the best reaction to have, considering.

John cursed the slow traffic. As shitty as he felt, he still wanted to get home and see Benji. He'd at least explain to Benji about being hurt over Benji's refusal to go with John to his parents' or church. John's phone rang and he darted a glance at the screen since he wasn't moving. Traffic was at a standstill. He recognized Dr. Hannah's office number and groaned. He'd never gone back and he'd meant to. He'd talked to Juleya the week before and promised to call back and schedule something.

"I'll do it tomorrow." John breathed a sigh of relief when the phone switched over to voicemail. The traffic began to creep along and by the time he got home, it was well after six. John ran up the stairs, eager to see Benji, and almost plowed over the man when he came flying out of the stairwell.

"Shit!" Benji yelped, stumbling backwards, arms flailing.

John grabbed for him, and they did a clumsy dance of tangled feet and arms. John hit the wall hard enough to make his shoulder ache, but he kept Benji and himself upright.

Benji grunted then started giggling.

"Glad you enjoyed that," John muttered.

Benji giggled again then grinned. "Well, I was going to run down and wait for you since you were late. I have good news, I think!"

John cocked his head and instead of telling him the news, Benji bounced up onto his toes and kissed him. It was a chaste kiss, but it was still better for them to do such things inside.

Benji tugged him along and waited while John unlocked and opened the door. "I need to get you your own key," John began, then hissed when he realized what he'd said, the implied seriousness of it.

"That'd be great." Benji touched his cheek, and looked at him with such appreciation it eased part of the burden John had been carrying. "I'd really like that, John. A lot. I know I was all about chasing dick before, but I'm really happy here, in this relationship."

John had to blink back the sudden burning in his eyes. "Me too."

Benji winked at him and went inside. "You could leave me the key tomorrow, and I'll have a copy made. Oh!" He spun around and fairly hopped in place. "Two things—I got the job!" He smiled so brightly it made John's jaws ache just seeing it. "I start Wednesday, and I'll be working days and nights, but nothing past eight because of Gramps." Benji's smile turned sly. "I told them I didn't want to disturb him because he's old and all, but I just want to be able to see you, too." He blushed and looked so sweet John had to kiss him, so he did.

"What's the second thing?" John asked, brushing his lips over Benji's.

"Uh." Benji closed his eyes then snapped them open. "Oh! This—" He pulled out his wallet, then opened it and took out a sheet of paper. "I know I need to get tested again to be sure, but it's a start, right?" Benji handed him the paper while John tried to breathe.

"You got tested?"

"Last week." Benji nodded. He bit his lip while John looked at the results. "I went to the clinic when you were at your parents' house. I hadn't been able to go sooner because gramps had doctor appointments every freaking day last week, all just regular stuff, but still. Sheesh."

"This is why you didn't want to go to my parents'?" John asked.

Benji averted his gaze and began toeing the carpet. "Mostly. I mean, I'm scared shitless to meet your family too, John. I'm not gonna lie to you. You make them sound so amazing, and they love you, and I'm just this little slut—"

"Stop that. Don't insult yourself, or me, or my family by implying you are anything other than the person I care for. They aren't judgmental assholes, Benji. They'll love you—" John just bit back the 'like I do' before he spewed it out. Now wasn't the time, and they both needed to know each other better before saying those words.

"Sorry."

"Congratulations on the job," John said, as neither of them seemed to have a clue what else to talk about at that point. "I bet you'll bring in a lot of tips."

Benji fluttered his lashes. "You're darn right I will." Then just as suddenly as he'd turned flirtatious, he stopped. "I promise, I won't fuck around, though. I won't, John. I know you don't have a reason to believe me—"

"Did you ever cheat on Derek?" John asked.

Benji moved back and scowled. "No, I wasn't the scumbag in that relationship."

"So why would I think you'd cheat on me?"

"Well." Benji pursed his lips and glared at him, then he dropped the act and all but dove into John's arms. "Yeah, you're right, smarty pants."

It felt so good to hold Benji, but John had to come clean. He wanted a good start in life for them together, not one built on any sort of dishonesty.

"I need to tell you something about last night, though. And…" John cleared his throat. "And the other time, when I first fucked you and it was—"

"Awesome." Benji sighed, looking up at him. "John, I know I hurt your feelings, and I realized what you were doing. I liked it. Pain-pain is a no-go for me, but like you do it? Just that little hint of a threat? Oh. My. God." Benji shivered and rubbed his erection against John. "See what it does to me, even thinking about it? So you can fuck me like that even when you aren't mad, you know. If I hadn't trusted you to stop if you hurt me, I'd never have let you do it."

"It was still wrong. I don't want to fuck you in anger—"

Benji cut him off with a loud snort that turned into a louder cackle. "Please. Angry sex is the *best* sometimes.

You think I won't be all over you trying to get you to let me top just because I need to pound out some anger? Maybe it won't be you I'm mad at, but I can see it. There's just something about fucking when you're mad, as long as you're not hurting your partner."

"You've done it before?"

Benji shook his head. "Nope, never topped. I've bottomed when I was mad and knocked Derek off the bed shoving backwards a time or two. I didn't feel bad either. So am I horrible?"

John couldn't even think about that, because what he wanted to know was something else entirely. "Will you fuck me?"

"Tonight?" Benji squeaked, eyes going round.

"Now," John clarified. He reached between them and began unbuttoning his shirt. "As soon as I can get naked. I'd like you to be the first — the only, Benji."

Benji's eyes were going to bug right out of his head. He fluttered and argued, but his cock was still hard and the tip had leaked, spreading a wet circle out on the denim.

"You said I had a *fine* ass. Don't you want it?" John turned around and shoved his slacks and briefs down, giving Benji a show.

"Oh my fucking hell," Benji muttered. "I'm gonna come before I even get my dick in there."

"You'd better not." John glared at him. "You'll last a lot longer if you come first, and I need to be able to walk and sit tomorrow at work without whimpering."

Benji's shy grin was the sweetest thing John had ever seen. He finished undressing and took Benji's hand. They walked into the bedroom and Benji removed his clothes while John got on the bed.

"How do you want me?"

Benji made a choked sound then answered, "It'll be easier on you if you're on your hands and knees. I'd love to fuck you face to face, but I don't think I'll last long enough to switch positions."

"Next time," John promised, and hoped he enjoyed it enough to keep his word.

"I'll make it perfect for you," Benji said as he pulled out a condom and lube. "I'm going to have to take my time stretching you because, well, I have a big dick and you have a little hole."

"Duh," John grumbled, getting to his knees.

"Hey."

John looked at Benji as he got on the bed. "Yeah?"

"How about I seduce you a little first?" Benji waggled his eyebrows.

John chuckled and flopped onto his side, opening his arms in offering. "Benji, you seduced me from the moment I saw you."

Benji winked at him then set down the lube and rubbers. He crawled over to John, straddling him, then kissed John with a fierceness he'd not yet experienced. Benji tended to be less aggressive than John when it came to kisses, or so John had thought. Not true, he realized, because Benji mastered John's mouth like he'd always owned it.

John was left making those same needy sounds Benji usually did. Benji nipped and licked his way down to John's neck.

"Wish I could mark you here," he muttered. He bit the spot.

"L-lower," John gasped, his cock beginning to perk up. "Collar."

"Oh yeah, baby," Benji cooed then he set his lips to the spot where shoulder and neck joined, and sucked.

John just about jerked out of his body, the pleasure fired through him so sharply. "God!"

"Just me," Benji said then he sucked again.

John began to quiver—parts of him did, at least. His thighs shook, the need to part them pressing. His arms did too, and he closed them around Benji's shoulders. Inside, he was gelatinous and warm, shaky and his hole—John had never been so aware of his own pucker in his life. It clenched and twitched and felt oddly empty.

"I have you," Benji told him. Then he moved down and started playing with John's nipples.

"Benji!" John shouted, his cock pulsing. "I'm gonna—"

"No you're not," Benji growled at him. "I will slap that dick of yours if it doesn't behave."

The threat, though John knew it was in jest, sounded awful and had him finding some self-control.

"Good." Benji sat up and got off him. "I'd give you some more foreplay but you're already too close to coming."

"I am," John rasped. He rolled over onto his hands and knees. "Fuck me."

"Right. Because I can just shove right on in and not make you feel like you're being plowed by a baseball bat."

"You're bigger'n that," John pointed out, pretty sure he was right.

Benji didn't answer. He just poured lube down John's crack and began rubbing it around his asshole.

"Oh. Oh, that's…" John didn't even have words for it. Benji's fingers were bringing to life every nerve ending down there.

"Good, huh?" Benji rubbed harder then slid the tip of one finger in.

John's eyes rolled back the second that digit went deep enough to touch his gland.

"So that's how you react to that," Benji mused. "I've heard some guys hate it."

John didn't give a ripe shit what other guys liked or hated, he just wanted more.

"Second one coming in."

"I don't need a play-by-play." John wiggled his hips. "Don't treat me like I'm gonna break."

Benji slapped his ass so hard John yelped and scrambled forward. "I'm doing it because I care about you and don't want you hurt!"

"So you beat my ass?" John snapped, exasperated and, embarrassingly, turned on.

Benji pointed to John's hard cock. "Didn't hurt you, did it?"

"It did hurt, but I liked it, if you want the truth." John pointed right back at him. "But not in that 'spank me, daddy' kind of way."

"Just the occasional swat," Benji said, nodding. "Gotcha. Now get your ass back over here. Wow. Look at that handprint!"

John rolled his eyes and got back in position. "Seriously, though, will you hurry up?"

"I won't risk hurting you, but I'll stop teasing."

John wondered about the truth of that promise minutes later as he was sobbing with a need to be fucked he couldn't contain. He undulated his hips, trying to ride the fingers fucking him.

Benji kept murmuring—John had no clue what he was saying as the words were so softly spoken. All John could hear was the thrumming of his own pulse and his heart beating in his ears.

Then Benji's fingers were gone and John was empty, empty. He groaned and tried to raise his head—only to moan as something thicker pressed into his ass.

"So good," Benji almost shouted. "Oh. My. Hell! I should have tried this with you sooner!"

John couldn't do anything but mewl as that thick cock sank into his ass. He felt stretched impossibly wide and he clenched around the invading shaft.

Benji yelled and grabbed his hips bruisingly hard. "Don't do that! Oh my God, I about came!"

John tried to be still, but he wanted that dick in deeper, and he wanted it the fuck out of him because, *Ow, even with prep that fucker hurts!* But it felt better more than it didn't, and Benji reached beneath him and fisted John's dick which felt even better-better.

"Aw, man, I'm not gonna last long at *all*," Benji whined. "You're gonna let me do this again, right?"

"Urgh." It wasn't the yes John had intended, but Benji's cockhead was rubbing over John's prostate and, *my God how am I supposed to speak!*

Benji grunted and rocked into him deeper and deeper, the angle of his dick keeping it in contact with John's gland more often than not. By the time Benji was fully seated in him, John was shaking and his legs were sliding farther apart.

Benji pulled back a little after a minute, then eased back in.

Fuck! Fuck, that's...that's so...so good! John couldn't even describe how good because Benji began thrusting, little movements first, while at the same time jacking John off. Then the movements became bigger, Benji withdrawing more and more, shoving back in harder and harder, jerking John's dick faster and faster.

John's head buzzed with a white noise and his vision hazed. He closed his eyes but bright spots of white and red kept bursting against his lids. He couldn't do anything but shove his ass up eagerly, needing every pounding thrust of Benji's cock.

Benji began cursing steadily, filthy words and things he wanted to do to John's ass. Some of them likely impossible, but hearing it turned John on so much he screamed in shock when his climax hit him.

"Ohmyfuckinghell!" Benji shouted, shoving in deep and dropping over John's back. "Fuck!" Words—more consonants than anything else—spilled from Benji's lips as he came. John was dimly aware of the swell of the cock in his ass, of the hot spurts filling the condom inside him. He wanted to feel that with nothing between them some day.

Benji whimpered louder than John did when he pulled his cock free of John's ass. "I'm dead," he groaned, collapsing beside John, who went down on his belly.

John grimaced. "Oh, yuch. Wet spot."

Benji snickered. "Scoot."

John took that to mean scoot closer to Benji, so he did. "Still nasty." He'd just smeared cum all over.

"Shower in a few minutes, then. Just let me drop into a coma now." Benji sighed and reached for his hand.

John wanted to relax, but he was sticky, and soon that'd turn to itchy, and his ass was definitely sore. None of that was what he said, though, because his brain apparently decided to have a spazz on him and make him ask, "Why wouldn't you go to church with me and Henry?"

Benji opened one eye and glared at him. "You're killing the afterglow, you ass. Because he's your friend and I figured that was y'all's thing. I can go next time if you want." Benji glared for another moment then closed his eyes again. "Ass."

John kind of liked the way Benji said it, all warm and affectionate, but still. "Gonna have to come up with another pet name. My mom won't care for that one at all, and she'll smack the crap out of you for saying it around her."

John got up and left Benji snarling at him. He was going to take that wonderful, grumbly, sweet man home with him, and tell his parents and siblings he'd finally found his Forever man.

About the Author

A native Texan, Bailey spends her days spinning stories around in her head, which has contributed to more than one incident of tripping over her own feet. Evenings are reserved for pounding away at the keyboard, as are early morning hours. Sleep? Doesn't happen much. Writing is too much fun, and there are too many characters bouncing about, tapping on Bailey's brain demanding to be let out.

Caffeine and chocolate are permanent fixtures in Bailey's office and are never far from hand at any given time. Removing either of those necessities from Bailey's presence can result in what is known as A Very, Very Scary Bailey and is not advised under any circumstances.

Bailey loves to hear from readers. You can find her contact information, website details and author profile page at http://www.pride-publishing.com.